I0719011

Presented To:

____

From:

____

On The Occasion

____

Contact Author at:
www.Gracereligiousbookspublishers.com

Business Office Phone: 1-203-891-7122

Copyright 2021 Grace Dola Balogun

The Trinitarian Activity Of Love

From Beginning Of Creation To Eternity

By Grace Dola Balogun

Grace Religious Books Publishing &
Distributors Inc. may be ordered through

Booksellers or by contacting the
publisher:

Grace Religious Books Publishing &
Distributors, Inc. New York

248 Lombard Street 2ndFloor
New Haven, CT 06513

All rights reserved. No part of this book may be used or

reproduced by any.

Means, graphic, electronic, or mechanical, including photocopying, recording,

Taping or by any information storage retrieval system without the written

Permission of the publisher except in the case of brief quotations embodied

In Critical articles and reviews: Because of the dynamic nature of the Internet,and web addresses, or links Contained in this book may have changed since publication and may no longer be valid. The views expressed in this work are solely those of the author and do Not necessarily reflect the views of the publisher, and the publisher hereby Disclaims any responsibility of them.

The author of this book does not dispense medical advice or prescribe the use

Of any technique as for treatment for physical, emotional, or medical problems

Without the advice of physician, either directly, or indirectly. The intent of the

Author is only to offer information of a general nature to help you in your quest

For emotional and spiritual well-being. In the event, you use any of the

Information in this book for yourself, which is your constitutional right, the

Author and the publisher assume no responsibility for your actions.

Scripture quotations marked (NIV) are taken from the Holy Bible, New International Version, NIV, Copyright 1973,1978,1984,2011 by Biblical,

Inc. Use by permission of Zondervan. All rights reserved

Worldwide. www.zondervan.com. The NIV and "New International version"

Are trademarks registered in the United States Patent and Trademark Office by Biblical, Inc. All other Scripture quotations, unless otherwise indicated, are taken from the King James Version of the Holy Bible. All Scripture quotations are used by permission. Scripture marked (NKJV) are taken from the New King James Version. Copyright 1982 by Thomas Nelson, Inc. Used by permission.

Also available in:

Soft Cover ISBN 978-1-939415-91-2

Hard Cover ISBN 978-1-939415-92-9

Library of Congress Control Number: 2021916623

Printed in the United States of America

Grace Religious Books Publishing & Distributor. Incorporated New York

The Trinitarian Activity Of Love

From

Beginning Of Creation To Eternity

Gen 1:1-2 Rev. 20:11

By

Grace Dola Balogun
Grace Religious Books
Publishing & Distributors,
Inc. NY

CONTENTS

Dedication

I dedicated This Book of the love and the activities of the Trinity! To God the Father, God the Son, and God the Holy Spirit Forever One God, through whom all things were created in Heaven and on this Earth. God the Father is the Architect, the planner, Son performs, and He carries out what the Father Planned. The Holy Spirit reveals and enforces what the Father planned and what the Son has performed. The Trinity work is teamwork; no member of the Godhead ever acts independently or acts out of synchronization with other members.

In addition to the great lesson of the teamwork of the Trinity we also learn what perfect obedience and total submission mean and look like. In the redemptive work, Father planned it, God the Son carried it out. He left His glory in Heaven and came down to the world, dying on the cross for our sins.

God the Father chose us, the Son redeemed us,

the Holy Spirit sealed us and empowered us; the Holy Spirit reveals the gospel into our hearts in creation the Spirit of God continuously moves over the face of the waters in this world even in this present moment. The Trinity is a towering, majestic doctrine of the Word of God from the Holy Bible; it also has a practical application in the lives of all the people in the world. As I start this book, I say, help us! Father, Son, and Holy Spirit as I dedicated this book unto you, the One God forever. May, we, all the believers, be able to operate in the same authenticity of teamwork as you the Trinity has done and continue to do in our lives. May we, as individuals, exhibit the same kind of submission and obedience to the Father as Jesus Christ did and He seated at the right hand of God. May the Holy Spirit continue to empower our hearts and in the minds of everyone on Earth. I'll put my best efforts in the purpose to let all those who will read this book acquire, recognize, obtained wisdom, knowledge, and understanding of the Trinitarian God's love for them. Bless them with perfect obedience, strong faith in you, and let them be converted into your Holy Hands. This Book is from You, it is for Your Glory and for the Exaltation of the Gospel of God on Earth as well as for the exaltation of the Holy Name of The Trinity One God Forever and Ever.

Preface

God created the Heaven and the Earth from the beginning of the creation and everything that dwells in it. Nothing in this world that has been created can escape the knowledge and recognition of God: The Holy Scriptures revealed an overview of the human beginnings from Adam to Abraham in the book of Genesis. I will keep my focus on this book on Five Events. God, the Almighty Father, is the creator of all things. He created the Sea, Sun, Moon, Stars, and Galaxy of Stars. He created the Animals, Fishes in the Ocean, and everything inside the Ocean. He created the Birds and everything that Crept on the ground. God created Adam and Eve in His own image and placed them in the Garden of Eden. The Book of Genesis revealed the love of God and the power of God for humanity step by step. The book of Genesis was the first book of the Holy Bible where God spoke and where we read about human history from the beginning of creation. In the book of Genesis, God revealed our own past; colored with human disobedience to God's word, human's sin, and then he blessed us with hope by showing us the way of redemption in the same book.

The Book of Genesis provides the essential foundation and preserves the trustworthy record about the beginning of the creation of the universe. It is where the details of the human race's sins have been revealed. The book blesses us with the stories of all the nations, male and female, ethnic groups, language. Even the life of Abram and the children of God who has been described in the truest of the forms. It beholds the love of God, the promise of God, as well as the promise of God to Abram, Isaac, and Jacob with a decree that never changes. God's purpose and His covenant will be fulfilled to his covenant people from the Old Testament to the New Testament.

The scripture revealed that: "In the beginning,

God created the Heavens and the Earth. Now the Earth was formless and empty darkness was over the surface of the deep, and the Spirit of God was hovering over the waters. The Lord God said;   "Let there be light, and there was light." (Genesis1: 1-3)

This means that God the three in one, one in three, the Holy Trinity One God, the True God within himself, and all that is divine brought something new into existence by his word. Just as His word became flesh and dwelled among us, it initiated a more significant blissful effect for his creation on Earth.

In His creation, God Almighty bring the nation of Israel into existence through Abraham. The Lord God's final action is going to be a New Heaven and a New Earth where righteousness will dwell forever. The Earth was formless; God the Father spoke it to be. God, the creator, is always and will always be now and forever - Amen. Since God the Holy Trinity is the source of all that exists, it proves that humanity and nature are not self-existent. In fact, they owe their life and their continuance to the Living God. God Almighty Father has a Sovereign right over all His creations by virtue of being the creator. The Earth was formless and empty, just as exactly how today, human beings' lives are empty with no meaning, formless, useless, without the presence of God in their hearts. Most of them had forgotten the absolute truth. Never was there a moment when God did not exist because God existed eternally and infinitely before the creation of the finite universe. God has revealed himself as a personal being that created Adam and Eve: "So God created man in his own image, in the image of God he created him; male and female he created them. God blessed them and said to them, "Be fruitful and increase in number; fill the Earth and subdue it; rule over the fish of the Sea and the Birds of the air and over every living creature that moves.

Then God said, "I give you every seed-bearing plant on the face of the whole Earth and every tree that has fruit with seed in it. They will be yours for food. To all the birds of the air and all the creatures that move on the ground and everything that has the breath of life in it -- I give every green plant for food" God saw all that He had made, and it was perfect. And there

was evening, and there was morning - the sixth day."
(Genesis 1:27-31)

The Trinitarian God had specific reasons and purpose for creating the world and human being to his own likeness. God the Father, Son, and God the Holy Spirit forever. God created the Heavens and the Earth as a manifestation of his glory, wisdom, power, and love. The Scripture revealed in the Book of Psalms of David: "The Heavens declare the glory of God; the skies proclaim the work of his hands. Day after day, they pour forth speech; night after night, they display the knowledge. There is no speech or language where their voice is not heard. Their voice goes out into all the Earth, their words to the ends of the world". (Psalm19:1-4) The Holy Scripture tells us that the physical world is a medium to declare and reflect God's glory, His love, and His creative power.

In another Scripture, we read: "O Lord, our Lord, how majestic, is your name in all the Earth! You have set your glory above the Heavens. From the Lips of children and infants, you have ordained praises because of your enemies to silence the foe and the avenger. When I consider Your Heavens, the work of your fingers, the moon, and the stars, which you have set in place, what is a man that you are mindful of him, the son of man that you care for him? You made him a little lower than the Heavenly beings and crowned him with glory and honor you made him ruler over the works of your hands; you put everything under his feet" (Psalm 8:1- 6)

This Scripture applies to the Son of Man, which is Christ Jesus. It is only in him that these truths are perfectly well acknowledged and come under the light of realization. Jesus Christ is the one who is the representative and the mediator between man and God. God the Father has given full dominion over all creation in Heaven and on Earth to Jesus Christ, His Son. Jesus Christ was given all power and authority over all the creations in Heaven and on Earth. Honor and glory were given to Jesus Christ when He came to us as the Son of God and the Son of man; God bestowed a tremendous honor through Jesus Christ on all humankind. We are created by God; for a glorious purpose. We are not just animals or the product of natural evolution, chance, or probability. We are so valuable to God; we are the object of his concern and favor.

God honored humanity by choosing us to be the ruler over his creations. It is not for us to be proud, but we must give praises and thankfulness and glory to the one and only - our Creator. God Almighty created the Heavens and the world in order to receive the glory and honor due to him. All the elements of nature, the Sun, the Moon, Trees of the Forest, Rain, Snow, Rivers and Streams, Hills, Mountains, Animals, Fishes in the Ocean, Birds of the air, and all the household pets must shout and give glory, honor, praise to the God who created them.

God also requires that all the human race must give glory to him as long as they live and have breathed. God created human race and the world in order to provide a place where His Will, His Purpose, and His goals for humanity can be manifest and fulfilled. God created all human race in his likeness so that He will have a loving relationship with them. A personal relationship with them; from this Earth to

Eternity.

God created the human being as a triune being - body, soul, and spirit. We are different from all other created beings; because we possess a mind that can go into the depths of God's wisdom and emotions that respond to His call.

Through our instincts and abilities, we are free in our worship. We are free to serve Him as our Lord God with unshakable strong, healthy faith, loyalty, and gratefulness. Our consciousness is a gift from Him that helps us maintained deep intimate relations with Him.

When Adam and Eve disobey God and his commandment, God promised to send a Savior, who is a redeemer, to redeem humanity from sin and death. In this way, those who belong to Jesus Christ and gave their lives to him automatically belongs to God and become God's possession. Those people are the ones who will enjoy God's glory and glorify him and live in his presence in righteousness and holiness in eternal life in Eternity forever.

The Scripture reveals: "Then I saw a new Heaven and a New Earth, for the first Heaven and the first Earth had passed away, and there was no longer any Sea. I saw the Holy City, the New Jerusalem, coming down out of heaven from God, prepared as a bride beautifully dressed for her husband. And I heard a loud voice from the throne saying, Now, the dwelling of God is with men, and He will live with them. They will be his people, and God himself will be with them and be their God." (Rev. 21:1-3)

The Scripture tells us that the final goal per God's desires and the Biblical expectation of all God's redeemed ones indicate a new transformation of the entire humanity. The redeemed ones of God, the born-again Christians on Earth, have a purpose. Also, under the Earth, where Jesus Christ dwells in the hearts of his people; in righteousness and in holy perfection. Their purpose is to erase all the forms and traces of sin from this present world because this Earth will be dissolved, and its elements will be destroyed. The new Heaven and the new Earth will become the dwelling place of both the human race and God. All the redeemed, born again, will possess an immortal body like the body that Jesus Christ's accumulated after the resurrection. Indeed the bodies that will be real, visible, and tangible, but they will be free of the corruption of all kinds - secured in an immortal shell forever.

The New Jerusalem exists in Heaven already, and it will soon descend down to Earth. It will dawn upon Earth as the City of God for which Abraham and all of God's had faithfully waited. It is a miracle for which God himself is the architect and the builder. The new Earth will become the dwelling place of God, and he will live and remain within his people. He will not be going back and forth anymore. God will stay permanently with his people forever, just as He planned it to be before Adam and Eve's disobedience in the Garden of Eden. There will be a new Heaven and a New Earth, one where there will be people of God and God himself will be with them, and He will forever be their God. The entire human race will be what God wants us to be. People of God will praise the Lord for his glory, honor, majesty, and adoration. There will be an abundance of praises and thankfulness for him forever till eternity and beyond.

His kingdom will have no end. The Prince of Peace will reign forever and ever. In the new Heaven and a New Earth, God's people will have full access to the "Tree of Life," the tree of the knowledge of good and evil was designed to test Adams's faith and obedience to God and his word and his commandment. God created humanity as a moral being with the ability to choose freely. Their choice included love and obedience towards their creator or to disobey and rebel against Him and His Will. God specifically imparted life and breath to the first man, unfolding profound wisdom in the phenomenon - the one that explains that human life stands higher and in a different category from all other forms of life. A unique relationship bounds the divine life to human life - God the Almighty is the ultimate source of human life. The creation of life to humanity is rightfully conceived as the result of a special act of God the Father, God the Son, and God the Holy Spirit in distinction from the creations of all other living beings.

Chapter One

The Trinity Before The Beginning Of Creation

God the Father, God the Son, and God the Holy Spirit existed before the foundation of the world. Their existence is from eternity and beyond. Jesus Christ is the incarnate Son of God. He lived with the Father because the Holy Scripture says: "In the beginning was the Word, and the Word was with God, and the Word was God. He was with God in the beginning. Through him, all things were made; without him, nothing was made that has been made. In him was life, and that life was the light of men. The light shines in the darkness, but the darkness has not understood it." (John 1:1-5)

Jesus Christ was the pre-incarnate Son of God and was united with the Father to partake in the Father's glory. Jesus Christ was pre-existent with God before the creation of the universe; He existed from eternity. His identity has a distinction from God the Father but is simultaneously entangled into an eternal fellowship with Him.

Jesus Christ is divine; the word of God has the same nature and essence as the Father. It was through Jesus Christ that God the Father created the Universe and continued to sustain it. Jesus Christ was not created. He is eternal, and He has always been in loving fellowship with God the Father and God the Holy Spirit. The Scripture revealed: "And God said, Let there be light, and there was light. God saw that the light was good, and he separated the light from the darkness." (Genesis 1:3-4)

God the Father referred to Jesus Christ as the life and the light bearer of the Universe. The primary purpose of the light is to separate the evil from good, to separate the work of Satan from the work of God. The light bearer will create a New Heaven and a New Earth because God the Father had already known what Adam and Eve were going to do before he created them. He knew that they would bring darkness to the world through Satan's deception, and they would disobey God's commandment.

God the Father knew that He would take the wisest of all decisions – sending His only begotten incarnate Son to the world in order to save the world, and that is why our Lord said: "And now, Father, glorify me in your presence with the glory I had with you before the world begun." (John 17:5)

All three members of the Trinity were active in the creation of the world. The Word of God, Jesus Christ the Creator and was with God the Father at the beginning. The Book of Colossians expounds on the supremacy of Jesus Christ: "He is the image of the invisible God, the firstborn over all creation. For by him all things were created; things in Heaven and on Earth, visible and invisible, whether thrones or powers or rulers or authorities all things were created by him and for him. He is before all things, and in him, all things hold together." (Colossians 1: 15-17) Jesus Christ is the heir and ruler of all creation as the eternal Son.

All things, may they be in the form of material and spiritual form, owe their existence to Jesus Christ's as He is the one who has always been an active agent in creation; within the blessings of Christ, all things in Heaven and on Earth are held together and sustained. Christ is the sustainer of this world, to whom all power and all dominion and authority belong. The first page of the Holy Scriptures in the book of Genesis gives us full and better satisfying wisdom and valuable knowledge of the beginning of the creation of the Universe.

God the Father is the maker of Heaven and Earth, Jesus Christ, and the Holy Spirit forever one God. He clearly indicates a plurality of presence in the Godhead: Father, Son, and Holy Spirit. The plural name of God speaks for himself as many though He is one, confirming our faith in the Holy Trinity. Since the beginning, God was always here. He existed before all ages, before time began, or before the beginning of time. The third person in the creation is the Holy Spirit. The Father said it, the Son carried it out, and the Holy Spirit empowers it.

The Spirit of God, the Father, is the Spirit of Jesus Christ, the Son. The Spirit of Jesus Christ is the Spirit of God, the Holy Spirit - one God forever and ever.

The Holy Spirit has an active role in the creation of the Earth. Each existence in the Trinity contributes to glorifying one another and having a triune relationship with each other. For example, our prayers bring glory to God the Father Almighty through Jesus Christ, our Savior. Our Lord said in the Scripture, "And I will do whatever you ask in my name, so that the Son may bring glory to the Father." (John 14:13)

When we pray in Jesus' Name, we are praying in harmony with his nature, character, and His Will; we are praying with faith in Him and His authority. Our prayers are uttered with a desire to glorify God the Father, Son, and the Holy Spirit. The Holy Spirit has an active role in the work of creation. The Scripture revealed that the Spirit of God roams over the Earth: "Now the Earth was formless and empty, darkness was over the surface of the deep, and the Spirit of God was hovering over the waters" (Genesis 1:2) the God Almighty Father, Son, and Holy Spirit forever one God has sovereign rights over all his creation by virtue of being the creator. He has the power over each existence and its destiny.

The Holy Spirit roams over the creation to preserve and protect the Earth for God the Father and the Son – it paves the path to imply their plan and further creative activities. Holy Spirit is the wind; and the breath of God. Just as breath of God is enough for us to make us alive when breathe on us. We become a living being when he takes away His breath we slumber back to being dust. This is the reason why the Psalmist affirms to us the role of the Holy Spirit: the Scripture says: "By the word of the Lord were the heavens made, their starry host by the breath of his mouth." (Psalm 33:6) The breath of God is the Spirit which also means the activity of the Spirit of God; the union of the power of the Word of God with the power of the Spirit of God: The Holy Spirit always releases the creative power of God's Spirit on behalf of his creations.

Likewise, in the book of Job, the Scripture reveals: "The Spirit of God has made me, the breath of the Almighty gives me life." (Job 33:4) The Holy Spirit is the giver of life proceeded with the blessings of the Father and the Son. It was the medium through the

Father, and the Son was worshipped, glorified, and adored. It spoke through the prophets and, to this day, still speaks to us. It dwells in every person's heart who are the believer of Jesus Christ. The Psalmist says: "When you send your Spirit, they are created, and you renew the face of the Earth." (Psalm 104:30)

The Holy Spirit is our comforter, Paraclete Heavenly guest who is still active in the life of all God's people and His creations on Earth in all the nations of the Earth. He will continue His creative work until Christ returns and set up His Kingdom of righteousness. The Spirit of God was the first mover; he moved upon the face of the waters, he began to work because God the Father Almighty created the world by his Spirit. The Holy Spirit moved upon the face of waters. God the Father is not the only author of the creation of the world and all beings; He is the fountain of life and the spring of motion. He commanded and created by his Spirit. God is preparing us for the New Heaven and the New Earth by the power of the Holy Spirit, which dwells in us, preaching, teaching, analyzing the Scripture. The Holy Spirit further leads all nations and all kinds of people to the gospel. Holy Spirit is an active agent in the New Earth, in collaboration with God the Father and God the Son.

God the Son reconciles us to God the Father through the power of the Holy Spirit, which is the Spirit of God - the Holy Trinity forever one God. Our Lord said: "If you love me, you will obey what I command. And I will ask the Father, and he will give you another Advocate, to be with you forever - the spirit of truth" (John 14:15)

Jesus Christ will ask the Father to give the Holy Spirit, which is the Advocate, to those who believe in him. He will speak for those who love him, follow his commandment, and focus on his word. The Spirit of God is great in power and mercy. He is our helper in times of Affliction, Distress, and Sadness. He strengthens believers in whatever they might be going through; He shows them the path of lives, holiness, and peace of God that transcends all understanding that is in Christ Jesus our Lord and Savior. Holy Spirit intercedes for us in our prayers and even delivers the prayers that never uttered through our lips.

Holy Spirit is our friend that never fails us, looking for our best interest constantly. The Holy light continuously directs us to the right path, to the way of peace, and holiness, and righteousness.

The Holy Spirit will remain with us forever from the life we spend on this Earth to the journey of Heavens that we will take. The Holy Spirit is called the Spirit of Truth; because he is a Spirit of Jesus Christ. It clarifies the way, the truth and the way of living the ultimate life for all humanity. The Spirit is an active agent before the creation of the world.

God the Father, God the Son, God the Holy Spirit will always be and forever will be in the Holy Trinity. There is and will always be One God from the beginning of all the planets and the world. Before the creation of the Earth, God Almighty experienced full satisfaction of himself. He dwelt joyfully among the spaces of His own creation happily alone in eternity as the Trinitarian God. Father, Son, and Holy Spirit the three Godhead were together in perfect harmony and fellowship with one another from all eternity. Holy, Holy, Holy, Lord God Almighty God in Three persons blessed the Trinity; God existed in three persons.

The Scripture clearly explained the activities of the Trinity in the following words: "Then God Said, Let make man in our image, in our likeness, and let them rule over the fish of the seas and the birds of the air; over the livestock, over all the Earth, and over all the creations that move along the ground" (Genesis 1:26)

The Lord God called all the three Godheads; by using "Let Us," which means God existed in three Godhead; this divine expression clearly indicates the involvement of the triune God. When God said, "Us," that means he is not the only one in the creation of the world.

Through these verses, He tells us about the particular plurality that He poses in his existence. He also beautifully explains specific details of creation how they work together in unity and with love. How God describes phenomena about the creation of human beings gives us more clarity about the nature of God Himself, what He has done, and what He is planning to do. Both males and females are special creations of God the Holy Trinity. The creation of males and females in God's image expresses a beautiful idea of equality. Human beings are created in the image of triune God, which depicts that they are relational beings.

Likeness in God's image indicates the physical similarity of the Trinity God. Human beings are God's image-bearer, also proving that males and female are not superior to one another. They both reflect the same equality to the character as God's creation.

The Lord God began His world by the power of His Spirit, which is the eternal light of the Spirit of God. The Holy Spirit shines on the formless and empty Universe with a striking impact so that by the Spirit of God's light, we may see the light on Earth and in our lives. This means through Jesus Christ, the light of the Holy Spirit blesses the soul of every Believer.

Jesus Christ, our Savior is the medium through which The Spirit of the Lord and the understanding of the gospel appeals to the believers.

It is the light of the Spirit of God that sparks up the Spirit, Soul, and Body of every man who comes to the world. The Spirit engaged in the creation from the beginning searches the human soul. God the Son is the Creator; He is also the Word of God without whom nothing is made and through whom the light of God reaches to the world. It was the Trinity that said, let us make man in our own image. It was Trinity that said, let there be light, and it was Trinity that created everything that exists in the world. Above all, it was Trinity that did the work of redemption and reconciled us towards themselves. It was both the Trinity that sent the Holy Spirit down to dwell in our hearts and mind; live the life of God through us, teaching us to live a Holy life. Through the Trinity, the New Heaven and the New Earth will come down to Earth. It will be through the Trinity that the Father, Son, and Holy Spirit will live with his people, and we will live with the Trinitarian God forever and ever.

The triune works at the creation of the world and says: "In the beginning, God created the Heavens and the Earth. The Earth was without form and void, and darkness was over the face of the deep. And the Spirit of God was hovering over the face of the waters." (Genesis 1:1-2)

The Biblical understanding of the work of redemption is at the heart of our Lord and Savior's claim, which says that this is eternal life. It says that the people must know the only true God, and Jesus Christ, whom God sent to tell about the triune God. This refers to the meaning of salvation in the Trinity which is the essential basis for our redemption.

It is to know the fact – the ultimate truth - that this world was one at the beginning of creation. It was created by infinite wisdom and power. It was created by the one who was present himself before all things and before all time and before all worlds.

Because of the difference between the creator and his creation, we realized that God manifests himself to us through his work of redemption. The Holy Spirit moved over the face of the water at the moment of creation; the Father made all things happen through the Son; nothing was created without the knowledge of the Son. All the Trinity works together in unity under one purpose and with the power of Love. Jesus Christ is one of the Triune God. He has no beginning and no end. Jesus Christ is one with the Father, and he said, "Before Abraham, I Was," (John 8:58) Jesus Christ always existed. He existed before all creations of the world. He is in the harmony of a beautiful bond with the Father, reflecting nothing but loving and in obedience with one another. Our Lord said: "My Father works, and I work" (John 5:17). We know that the trinity is always working to make this world a better place to live.

Chapter Two

Father, Son, And Holy Spirit One God

God the Father, God the Son, and God the Holy Spirit are always together as one infinite compassionate existence; all-powerful and Almighty God; One God forever and ever. In the creation of Heaven, and the Earth, Father, the Son, and the Holy Spirit are together. It was because the Spirit of God the Father is the Spirit of God the Son, and The Spirit of God the Father, Son is the Spirit of God that created; the same Spirit is divided severally according to his purpose, and according to His Will. God the Father, Almighty spoke the Heaven and the Earth into existence. The Trinity has involved: the Father was not alone. In His infinite power, God spoke the Earth into being with the power of His work. The Earth was full of darkness and emptiness. The Spirit of God was moving over the waters, the same Spirit of God spoke and said, "let there be light," (Genesis 1:3) and the light came down and pierced through the darkness. That light is the

Spirit of Jesus Christ that came down from Heaven, and it lit the world.

The Almighty God brings all things together out of nothing - God exists as three but is one in Spirit. There was no pre-existent matter out of which the Earth was made; the Earth was empty and formless; God created the universe by His Spirit that was hovering over the Earth. He spoke through the same Spirit using His infinite power. God said, let there be light, and the light appeared, shining in the darkness. The darkness cannot overpower it. The Almighty Father is the foundation of life and the joy of motion; otherwise, the Earth might still be empty and formless even to this day.

The same God who spoke to prophet Ezekiel and raised all the dead bones to life in the valley of dry bones as per the holy Scripture, which revealed: "The hand of the Lord was upon me, and he brought me out by the Spirit of the Lord and set me in the middle of a valley; it was full of bones. He led me back and forth among them, and I saw a great many bones on the floor of the valley, bones that were very dry. He asked me, Son of man, can these bones live? I said, O Sovereign Lord, you alone know. Then he said to me, Prophesy to these bones and say to them, Dry bones, hear the word of the Lord! This is what the Sovereign Lord says to these bones: I will make breath enter you, and you will come to life. I will attach tendons to you and make flesh come upon you and cover you with asking; I will put breath in you, and you will come to life. Then you will know that I am the Lord. So I prophesied as I was commanded. And as I was prophesying, there was a noise, a rattling sound, and the bones came together, bone to bone. I looked, and tendons and flesh appeared on them, and skin covered them, but there was no breath in them. Then he said to me, Prophecy to the breath; prophesy, son of man, and say to it. This is what the Sovereign Lord says: Come from the four winds, O breath, and breathe into this slain, that they may live. So I prophesied as he commanded me, and breath entered them; they came to life and stood up on their feet a vast army." (Ezekiel 37:1-10)

God the Father, the Son, and The Holy spirit forever

one God through his Spirit spoke to the prophet Ezekiel raised up the dead, dry bones in the Valley and spoke life and breath into them so that they may live and worship him. Spirit of God was upon prophet Ezekiel in a vision, and He saw a valley full of dead, dry bones. These bones represented the entire house of Israel, including Judah in exile, whose hope had died when they were dispersed among foreigners. It happened because of the disobedience and sins that they committed. God led prophet Ezekiel to prophesy of the bones, and the bones were raised to life again. They were raised to live again in two different ways. One, they were politically and physically restored to their land; two: God's infinite power enabled the spiritual restoration of their faith in God; God's infinite power restored them. The restoration of the people of Israel to life reminded all the human race of what God the Father did in the creation of the Universe. It reminded them how, when the Earth was empty and formless, the Spirit of God created the Earth by his Word. He spoke the Earth to existence.

He spoke, and Adam's physical existence was

formed, then God breathed on him the ultimate breath of life. In a similar manner, the people of Israel were dead and lost in their sins and trespasses. God restored them physically and then gave them his breath of life by pouring out his spirit upon them. The Father, Son, and the Spirit still work together in the New Life in Christ Jesus. The Father is the planner; He is the architect, the teamwork of God. The Trinity is incomparable; the Father plan, the Son carry it out, the Holy Spirit empowers it. The Son performs. He carries out what the Father planned. The Holy Spirit reveals and enforces what the Father and the Son have planned and performed. No member of God's head works alone or acts independently or does anything without the other members in the Trinity.

In the work of redemption, the Father planned the redemptive work, God the Son carried it out by dying on the Cross. Christ Jesus made a statement in the Garden of Gethsemane, where Jesus prayed before his crucifixion. The Holy Scripture revealed" "Going a little farther, He fell with his face to the ground and prayed, My Father, if it is possible, may this cup be taken from me. Yet not as I will, but as you Will. " (Matthew 26:39)

When Jesus Christ was in agony at the Garden of Gethsemane, the Father and the Spirit were together with him; Jesus, the Son, was not alone. The Son was praying to be saved from physical death. However, it was planned and set by the Father as He had to die for the sins of the human race.

He prayed to be delivered from the punishment of separation from God the Father because of the ultimate penalty for humanity's sin. Jesus, the Son of God, prayed that His physical death was accepted and atoned as full payment for the whole world's sin.

He prayed that God the Father's Will be done, not His own Will. His obedience to the Father's should be our example; because he committed himself entirely to go through the physical death and the spiritual separation from the Father and the Holy Spirit so that He could achieve our salvation as per the plans of His Heavenly Father.

The Son's prayer was heard, and His Father

strengthened Him in order to be able to drink the appointed cup. We see here clearly that the Father planned, and the Son carried out the work of redemption. The redemptive work was completed through our Lord Jesus Christ forever. We see the Father's action and plan in the Holy Scripture revealed: "For God so loved the world that he gave His one and only Son, that whoever believes in Him shall not perish but have eternal life. For God did not send His Son into the world to condemn the world, but to saved the world through Him." (John 3:16-17)

God the Almighty, the master planner, loved the world so much that he sent his only incarnate begotten Son into the world. This Scripture reveals the heart and purpose of God in Heaven.

The God the Holy Trinity all three are in combined power. The love of God is wide enough to embrace all the people of this universe. God, the Almighty Father, gave His Son as an offering for our sin on the cross. The atonement precedes the loving heart of God the Father.

It is something that was not forced on the Son to do; it is the loving will of the Trinity. God the Father, God the Son, and God the Holy Spirit one God did not want anyone to perish. He wanted them to be enlightened to the knowledge of repentance and pray for the forgiveness that was only accessible through Christ Jesus the God's Son and the only Savior for all the people on Earth.

By our full assurance, trust and faith in the Son, He will bring us to grace and salvation as well as to fellowship with God the Father in the unity of the Holy Spirit in Heaven. God Almighty showed his love to humanity when he sent his Son to the world to attain redemption and the salvation of the human race. God the Father gave His only begotten Son, gave Him up to suffer and die for us. No one, not even the enemies, would have been able to take Him if the Father did not give Him to them as a sacrifice for human sins.

Therefore, God has commended His love to the people of this world; the Holy God loves us, died for the wicked and unholy; for our present, past, and future sins. Christ was first sent to come to the Jewish people only, but now through Jesus Christ the incarnate Son of God; Salvation reach all the people on Earth, Jews and the Gentile. Through Jesus Christ's Salvation came to everyone on Earth. Whoever believes in Jesus Christ shall not perish; God has taken away their sin, they shall not die, Christ has purchased them with His pressures blood.

All those who believe; in the Son and gave their lives to him will enjoy eternal life in Heaven; they shall have everlasting life. God designed it and sent his Son into the world; so that the world through him might be saved. Jesus Christ came to the world with Salvation in his eyes. He entered the world with the gift of grace and salvation in his hand. God sent his begotten Son into the world as his agent or as his ambassador. He was a resident who did not come to condemn the world but to save it. The Scripture reveals: "This is my command: Love each other. If the world hates you, keep in mind that it hated me first. If you belonged to the world, it would love you as its own. As it is, you do not belong to the world, but I have chosen you out of the world. That is why the world hates you. Remember the words I spoke to you: No servant is greater than his master. If they persecuted me, they persecute you also. If they obeyed my teaching, they obey yours also. They will treat you this way because of my name, for they do not know the One who sent me." (John15: 17-21)

Our Lord and Savior made it clear here that the Father is the one that sent Him here to the world. As they do not know the Father, it is hard for them to know the Son. The true believers of Jesus Christ must have the knowledge of the people of the universe; the false prophets, people of all other religions, the Idol worshipers and Pagans. Some churches always opposed the things of God, and then there were churches that did not want anything to do with the cross of Christ. Then there are those who opposed God and the principles of his kingdom. Therefore, they will continue to be an enemy and haters of God and haters of the cross of Christ.

They will Persecute the faithful believers till Christ returns to judge the dead and the living. The Father, the Son, and the Holy Spirit sent his Son to the world with the Holy Spirit. The Scripture revealed: "In the sixth month, God sent the angel Gabriel to Nazareth, a town in Galilee, to a virgin pledged to be married to a man named Joseph, a descendant of David. The virgin's name was Mary. The angel went to her and said, Greetings, you who are highly favored! The Lord is with you. Mary was greatly troubled at his words and wondered what kind of greeting this might be. But the angel said to her. Do not be afraid, Mary; you have found favor with God. You will be with child and give birth to a son, and you are to give him the name Jesus. He will be great and will be called the Son of the Highest. The Lord God will give him the throne of his father David, and he will reign over the house of Jacob forever; his kingdom will never end. How will this be, Mary asked the angel, since I am a virgin? The angel answered. The Holy Spirit will come upon you, and the power of the Highest will overshadow you. So the Holy one to be born will be called the Son of God." (Luke1: 26-35)

We see here how the Father, the Son, and the Holy

Spirit teamed together in the work of redemption by speaking the Son into being in the womb of the Virgin Mary. It happened just as the Spirit was moving on the face of the water, and the Spirit of God the Father was given life in the womb of Virgin Mary, the Son of God. Virgin Mary was chosen above all women on the Earth to be the birth mother of Jesus Christ the Messiah. Virgin Mary was chosen because she found favor with God. Her humbleness and faithfulness, godly life pleased God more than any other woman on Earth during that time. God was happy with her to the extent that she was chosen by the Father to carry out this important task. All the Christian believers must make themselves available to be used for the glory of God from this Earth to Heaven.

The Spirit of God that hovered over the Earth and came upon Mary, God's very Spirit arrived in the womb of Virgin Mary. This is why the apostle John says: "In The beginning was the Word and the Word was with God, and the Word was God. He was with God in the beginning. Through him, all things were made that has been made. In him was life, and that life was the light of men. The light shines in the darkness, but the darkness has not understood it." (John 1: 1-5)

Jesus Christ was with the Father from the beginning of creation. Jesus is the word of God, spoken into the Virgin Mary's womb, and He became man and dwelled among us. We behold his glory, the glory of one and only incarnate begotten Son of God. Jesus Christ is the personal Word of God; Jesus Christ is the manifold wisdom of God the Father Almighty. Jesus Christ is the perfect revelation of nature, and he is the person of God; just as the person's words reveal his or her heart and mind, Jesus Christ reveals through God's powerful Word.

The main characteristic of God is that Christ Jesus is the Word of God in relation to the Father. Christ Jesus was pre-existent with God before the creation of the world or before God spoke the World into existent. Christ was one and only existing from eternity; He is God's eternal forever one God. Christ was in eternal fellowship with the Father. Jesus Christ was divine. The Word was God having the same nature and essence as the Father. Jesus Christ was the word of God in relation to the world; it was through Jesus Christ the Father created and sustained the world. Jesus Christ is the word of God in relation to all the people on Earth; the Word became flesh just as we are and lived with us for 33-years.

The Son of the highest God took on human nature, lived with us, and ate with us without sin. He put on our likeness. He was the Son of God and the Son of Man that live on this Earth sinless. Jesus Christ came down from Heaven and entered the condition of humanity's life through the Virgin Mary who gave human birth, and yet it was the birth of the Son of God. Jesus Christ was not created. He is divine and eternal, always in perfect obedience and fellowship with the Father and the Holy Spirit one God forever.

The Father chose us; the Son redeemed us, the Holy Spirit sealed us. In addition to the great lesson of teamwork from the Father, Son and Holy Spirit, we also learn what the perfect obedience and submissions look like. The Scripture revealed in the Holy Bible when Jesus said: "Then Jesus came to them and said, all authority in Heaven and on Earth has been given to me. Therefore go and make disciples of all nations, baptizing them in the name of the Father and the Son and of the Holy Spirit, and teaching them to obey everything I have commanded you. And surely I am with you always, to the very end of the age." (Matthew 28: 18-20)

Jesus Christ, before his ascension, promised us the authority and power to proclaim the gospel throughout the world. However, the condition is to first obey the gospel and Jesus Word. Christ's command them to wait for the promise of the Father, which is the power of the Holy Spirit at the Pentecost. We must have the power of the Holy Spirit to accompany our work. We must have the strength to spread the Word of God to all the nations so that we can keep preaching, teaching, proclaiming the gospel. Without the manifestation of the Holy Spirit, it is impossible to serve faithfully without the interruption of enemies.

The preaching and the teaching of the gospel must be centered on repentance and forgiveness of sins. By receiving the gift of the Holy Spirit, we will be able to serve with confidence. The Holy Spirit will be helping, teaching and directing our path, step by step, in everything we do for the Lord as we wait for the Lord's return from Heaven. The Holy Spirit manifestation will help us and empower us to fulfill the great commission, converts the human souls and observe Jesus Christ's commandment. Spiritual energies must not be concentrated only on making and counting the number of the congregation. The act must be based and observed according to the conversion of the souls as Christ commands us to reach the sinners and the lost and makes disciples from all the nations. The Holy Spirit is the giver of life, who proceeded from the Father and the Son.

Through the Father and the Son, he was worshipped and glorified; he spoke through the prophets and continues to speak to us till today. The Holy Spirit empowered the apostles on the day of Pentecost. He gave them the utterance to speak and understand all the languages of the people from all other nations that were in Jerusalem on that day.

Our Lord said, "All this I have spoken while still with you. But the Advocate, the Holy Spirit, whom the Father will send in my name, will teach you all things and will remind you of everything I have said to you. Peace I leave with you; my peace I give you. I do not give to you as the world gives. Do not let your hearts be troubled and do not be afraid." (John 14:25-27)

Holy Spirit teaches us to read the Holy Bible and be a doer of the word of God, not hearer alone. The Holy Spirit teaches us the word of God, along with the manifestation of godly Character, in the lives of all the believing Christians, which is the most important to all the Christians as we are the body of Christ. Holy Spirit is the Paraclete heavenly guest who is with the Father and the Son. He was honored and glorified and will live in our hearts forever. Holy Spirit is our helper, or spokesperson, one that come to us to help us.

Our Lord said in another Scripture that he would send a helper, as a friend who comes to us to help us in everything we might be going through. Someone like Him; just as Jesus was in deed the helper of disciples during his Earthly ministry. "Jesus left the Synagogue and went to the home of Simon. Now Simon's mother-in-law was suffering from high fever, and they asked Jesus to help her. So he bent over her and rebuked the fever, and it left her. She got up at once and began to wait on them." (Luke 4:38-39) NIV

Whenever the disciples were filled with hopelessness, or whenever they were tired, confused or at odds with one another, Jesus Christ would give them his unfailing help, teaching and performed a miracle. Christ is always there when the apostle needs him. That was the reason Christ told the apostles that it is better that He go away because by going away, He will be able to send the Paraclete heavenly guest to the people that will abide with them forever. The Holy Spirit will bring the believers closer to Jesus and make His power available whenever they need it. Where ever they may be, or whatever they are doing; The Holy Spirit, the Spirit of God the Father and the Son will live in the hearts and minds of all the believers.

The Holy Spirit and our great intercessor will

intercede in our prayers and will make us strong in faith. We will be able to emphasize a consistent attitude of love for the Father, Son and the Holy Spirit and be obedient to His Holy Word and His commandments.

Without the power of the Holy Spirit, no one can live a Christian life that the Lord requires from us. Holy Spirit will come to believers in all situations of life and pray for them, the prayer that cannot be uttered. Here we can see that the Father, Son and the Holy Spirit: are always forever one God One in essence.

The Scripture in the book of Hebrew says that God the Son radiates God the Father's glory because Christ shares God the Father's nature and essence. We must know that whatever God the Father is in His character and nature, Jesus Christ is the same. Christ is the exact representation of God the Father.

Therefore, the revelation of God himself is no longer fragmentary or incomplete as in the Old Testament. Jesus Christ, the true and Holy Son is the revelation of the Father in fullness and completeness. In Christ, God the Father's revelation and his prophetic Word came literally in many ways and paths to us. Where; some paths are in the Old Testament; in order to add up to the fullness of what God had to say to us. But now God the Father has spoken as well as revealed himself to humanity by his Son Jesus Christ in a full and complete way because Jesus Christ is the supreme over all things.

The World of God through him is complete and final. So it transcends all the previous Words by God and humanity. Jesus Christ, the true Son of God by whom all things are Complete; Jesus Christ's manifestation journey began from the Old Testament to the New Testament. The Scripture reveals: "By the seventh day God had finished the work he had been doing. So on the seventh day he rested from all his work. And God blessed the seventh day and made it holy" (Genesis 2:2-3)

After God Almighty finished all the work of creation, He blessed the seventh day for both physical and spiritual reasons and as a memorial to the completion of His created work. The meaning of rest from all His work is like when a lawyer rests a case, he or she ceases the arguments, so, similarly, God ceased from his creative work. He is now creating new universes. God did not rest on the seventh day of creation for His own sake, but for our sake.

God himself modeled the seventh day's rest principle because of its utmost importance for our spiritual, physical, mental and emotional wellbeing.

Rest renews our minds, our Souls, and our Bodies. If we do not rest, our bodies will become tired, and we might also lose the edge of our mental keenness and creative energy; this way, our lives might become less productive. God Almighty Father sanctified one day of the week to rest as a day of blessing for every person in the world.

God gave the seventh-day principle of rest so much importance spiritually and physically that He added it on the Ten Commandments for his covenant people. This shows how caring and loving our Lord is to us. God cared about our well-being so much that He put the seventh day as part of His commandment. Like a Father, he cares for us; He wants us to be in good health and full of energy. God Father, Son and Holy Spirit want us to have a good relationship with Him right from the beginning of creation. He brought all the animals to Adam to give them their name. He always used to come down to the Garden of Eden and walk with Adam and Eve before the fall.

He would walk with them and talk to them and tell them about His love for them. God Almighty maintains His direct relationship with His people or nature. He always develops loving relationships with human beings. He is the all-powerful creator.

The Scripture reveals: "Then the man and his wife heard the sound of the Lord God as he was walking in the garden in the cool of the day, and they hid from the Lord God among the trees of the garden. But the Lord God called to the man, "where are you" He answered, I heard you in the garden, and I was afraid because I was naked, so I hid. And he said, who told you that you were naked? Have you eaten from the tree that I commanded you not to eat from? The man said, the woman, you put here with me - she gave me some fruit from the tree, and I ate it. Then the Lord

God said to the woman. What is this you have done? The woman said the serpent deceived me, and I ate. Then the Lord God said to the woman. What is this you have done? The woman said the serpent deceived me, and I ate. So the Lord God said to the serpent, because you have done this, cursed are you above all the livestock and all the world animals you will crawl on your belly, and you will eat dust all the days of your life." (Genesis 3:8-14)

Adam and Eve broke the good loving relationship between them and God by disobeying the commandment of God. They both ran away from the presence of God because of their sins. The Lord God drove them out of the garden.

He did not come down to walk with them, talk to them in the garden anymore because they ran away from the presence of the Lord. They broke the covenant relationship, but God still showed them love, by clothing them with the skin of an animal which is the first sacrificial shed blood for sin. Up till today, the Lord God still calls us for a good relationship with Him through Christ Jesus our Lord. Up till today,

God the Father, Son and Holy Spirit still visit us and shower His infinite love upon us.

All the fullness of God the Father Almighty is in the Lord Jesus Christ. Christ is the first to be raised from the dead into the glory of God, he is our resurrected Lord, and Christ is coming again to set up His Kingdom of peace and righteousness. "The Son is the radiance of God's glory and the exact representation of his being, sustaining all things by his powerful word. After he had provided purification for sins, he sat down at the right hand of the Majesty in Heaven." (Hebrew 1:3)

The Scripture of the book of the Hebrews was based on Jesus Christ deity, his priesthood; Christ is our High Priest in Heaven and on Earth. His sacrificial power, Jesus Christ, paid the ransom for our sin on the cross.

He sacrificed himself for us, so those of us that we live do not live for ourselves, but for him, who loves us and gave his life for us, we must live for him forever in Christ glory.

Christ Jesus ascended into Heaven and back

to his glory. God spoke through all the prophets, Moses, Abraham; but God's full and final revelation is through His Son Jesus Christ, and the revelation is absolute, valuable, authoritative, Christ is the heir of all things, the more manifest of God's Will, God the Father has committed all the work of creation into Christ Holy Hands, Jesus Christ is the radiance of God's very nature; the radiance of the glory of God, he is the exact representation representing God the Father on this Earth.

Christ is the revealer of God. God is in Jesus Christ reconciling the people of the world into Himself. Jesus Christ is the one that upholds all things by his powerful Word, and he is in control now and forever. Jesus Christ is suffering at the place of authority and power at the right hand of God the Father and reigns in the unity of the Holy Spirit one God forever. Jesus Christ is the eternal Son of God; God the Father said: "You are my Son; today I have become your Father." (Psalm 2:7) Christ Jesus is the true Son of God who came down from Heaven in our likeness to reconcile us to God so that we can be able to call God "Abba father" The Scripture says: "By the Word of God the Heavens were made, their starry host by the breath of his mouth" (Psalm 33:6) The Word of God is God and is right. The word of God can be trusted, the Word of God is powerful, and the hands of God and his word manifest his great power in the foundation of the world. "Through him all things were made; without him nothing was made that has been made." (John1: 3)

Jesus Christ is the eternal word of God; the word of God has no end. Christ Jesus have an intimate relationship with God the Father, Jesus Christ is divine. He is God in human flesh, God in flesh magnified. The Word was God; he is the creator of the Earth Jesus Christ is the revelation of God; just as God spoke the Earth into existence God spoke Christ into being into the womb of Virgin Mary, with the power of the Holy Spirit. The Scripture says: "Father, I want those you have given me to be with me where I am, and to see my glory, the glory you have given me because you loved me before the creation of the world." (John 17:24)

All the believing Christians must love each other as Christ loved all of us. In order to be in unity for the work of the Lord the work of the Lord we must love each other. God almighty demonstrated his love for us, by sending his only begotten Son to the world, to take away our sin. We must love as Christ love. Christ Jesus wants the Father to be glorify in everything he is doing, we Christians must follow the example of Jesus Christ and let everything we do or say bring glory to his Holy name Jesus Christ pray for us before he leave the Earth, he pray for our sanctification and the power of the Holy Spirit indwelling in our lives. We are the body of Christ, Christ is the head of the church, He is the foundation of the church, we are part of His body, His flesh and His bones, and we must live a life that will bring great glory to His holy name.

SECOND COMING OF CHRIST

After the second coming of Jesus Christ at the end of the age; the Children of Israel and all the nations will be rebuilt and all other nations will work together among themselves and worship the Lord with them.

Israelites will function as priests and ministers, teaching and preaching on meditating the word of God to unconverted people in all the nations of the Earth. When Christ returns, all who belong to him will greatly be delighted and rejoice in him; they will automatically be a part of his kingdom of righteousness. They will be clothed with the garments of salvation and praise. They will belong to God's redemption, and a robe of righteousness will be given to them. They will live by the standard of God, forever. Jesus Christ showed the disciples his heavenly glory as the Scripture reveals: "After six days Jesus took with him Peter, James, and John the brother of James, and led them up a high mountain by themselves. There he was transfigured before them. His face shone like the sun, and his clothes became as white as the light. Just then there appeared before them Moses and Elijah, talking with Jesus. Peter said to Jesus, Lord, it is good for us to be here. If you wish, I will put up three shelters one for you, one for Moses, and one for Elijah. While he was still speaking a bright cloud enveloped them, and a voice from the cloud said: "This is my son, whom I love; with him, I am well pleased, listen to him". When the disciples heard this, they fell facedown to the ground, terrified. But Jesus came and touched them. Get up, he said don't be afraid. When they looked up, they saw no one except Jesus." (Matthew 17:1- 8). In his transfiguration, Jesus Christ was transformed in the presence of his three disciples, Peter, John, and James, and they saw Jesus Christ's heavenly glory as he was, which is God in human flesh. The experience of the transfiguration of Christ was (1) an encouragement to Jesus as he faced death on the cross. (2) It was an announcement to the disciples that Jesus Christ had to suffer on the cross which was an endorsement by God, the Father that Jesus Christ was his true Son qualified to redeem the human beings from sin and death. Raising Lazarus from the dead was the last miracle of Jesus Christ. It was a miracle that displays the power of God. It was also an unmistakable sign that Jesus was the Christ, the Messiah. Therefore, many of the Jews, who came to Mary and Martha; saw what Jesus did, and they truly believed that he is the Messiah. The Pharisees and Sadducees beginning to find a way to kill Him. But for those who have faith in him, it was the beginning of a new life in

Jesus. Raising Lazarus demonstrated the true nature of Jesus Christ; it exemplifies Christ's authority over sin and death. The most important was about the manifestation of Jesus Christ's power that reached the grave and raised the dead. This demonstrates the power that cleansed us from our sin's bondage and blessed us with a new life in him by making us a new creature; it also demonstrates the love of Jesus Christ that made him come down from heaven to redeemed humanity from their sins and reconciled them to God, the Father. It helps those who gave their lives to Jesus Christ to know his glory, his power to save, and his presence. Jesus Christ always visits the house of Mary and Martha in Jerusalem where they both live with their brother Lazarus. They know him as their friend, not just as a stranger but a true friend, this shows the human side of Jesus Christ; they were used to Christ's loving care for them; his fellowship and his presence. Jesus Christ is still the same to those who love him and maintain a close re-lationship with him up till today. His loving care nev-er fails and never ceases. When Jesus Christ delays in answering the prayer that means he wants to do greater things in our lives that no one can imagine. Believers need to continue growing and to continuing strengthened their belief in him.

Chapter Three

The First Time The Trinity Visited The Earth After The Flood

The Lord God, the Trinitarian God always visited Adam and Eve and walked with them in the Garden of Eden. But after the fall he did not visit the earth until after the flood to protect, correct, and settle them in their planned location. The Trinity came down to see what they were planning to do.

The Lord God Almighty Father visited the earth after the flood, where God settled down Noah and his family. The Holy Bible says: "The region where they lived stretched from Mesha towards Sephar, in the eastern hill country. These are the sons of Shem by their clans and languages, in their territories and nations. These are the clans of Noah's sons, according to their lines of descent, within their nations. From these the nations spread out over the earth after the flood." (Genesis 10:30-32) After their settlement, they continued to grow and said to themselves: "Now, the whole world has one language and a common speech." As men moved eastward, they found a plain in Shinar and settled there. They said to each other, "Come, let's make bricks and bake them thoroughly." They used brick instead of stone, and tar for mortar. Then they said, "Come let us build ourselves a city, with a tower that reaches the heavens, so that we may make a name for ourselves and not be scattered over the face of the whole earth." But the Lord came down to see the city and the tower that the men were building. The Lord said, if the people speaking the same language have begun to do this as one, then nothing they plan to do will be impossible for them. "Come, let us go down and confuse their language, so they will not understand each other. So, the Lord scattered them from there over all the Earth, and they stopped building the city. That is why it was called Babel -- because there, the Lord confused the language of the whole world. From there, the Lord scattered them over the face of the whole earth."(Genesis 11:1-9) God the Father, the Son, and the Holy Spirit are always together in all the intervention of what is going on in the world, there is no time that they did not get involved with what we are doing to ourselves, individually and to ourselves nationally. There is subordination within the Trinity. Scripture shows that the Holy Spirit is subordinate to the Father and the Son, and the Son is subordinate to the Father. This is an internal relationship and does not deny the deity of any Person of the Trinity. This is simply an area that our finite minds cannot understand concerning the infinite God. The place was called Babel-- because there the Lord confused the language of the whole world. From there, He scattered them over the face of the whole earth. The people of Noah's day after the flood did the same thing that Adam and Eve did by eating from the fruit of knowledge and evil; The Scripture revealed: "And the Lord God said, the man has now become like one of us, knowing good and evil. He must not be allowed to reach out his hand and take also from the tree of life and eat, and live forever. So, the Lord God banished him from the Garden of Eden to work the ground from which he had been taken. After he drove the man out, he placed on the east side of the Garden of

Eden Cherubim and a Flaming of sword flashing back and forth to guard the way to the tree of life." (Genesis 3:22-24) Adam and Eve wanted to be God, they had attempted to set themselves up as God's equal and to determine their standards, they did not want to follow the commandment of God. Through their fall, people of this world became independent of God as they distinguished for themselves between good and evil. They said to themselves whatever makes you happy go ahead and do that. In this world, imperfect and perverted human judgment often decides what is good and evil. This is not the Will of God to all human beings. God intended humanity to know only good in dependence on him and his word. Because of Adam and Eve's sin of disobedience, their perfect relationship with God was lost. God drove them out of the Garden of Eden, and a life of dependence on God amid all the earthly trials and tribulations began and Satan the deceiver gained power over the world. God almighty that has an infinite love for the people of this world is so much determined to conquer Satan by reconciling the people of this world back to himself through Jesus Christ, his only begotten Son. When sin polluted the world, the Lord God Almighty wanted to destroy the world but found one righteous man Noah. He decided to save the world by starting a new world through Noah and his descendant. After the flood, the people of the world continued to multiply and increase. The Lord God Almighty established his covenant with humanity and nature in which he promised, never again to destroy the earth and all the living creatures with flood anymore; He gave a sign of the rainbow as an ongoing reminder of his promise, never again to destroy all the inhabitants of the earth by flood. The sign of the rainbow reminds us of his mercy and faithfulness to his Word. Humans started planning again as they grew and wanted to make themselves equal with God. They said to themselves let us build a tower and make a name for ourselves. The sin of the people by their desire was to dominate the world and make their destiny apart from God. The purpose was based on pride and rebellion against the commandment of God. This made the Lord come down and check out the City, where the Tower of Babel had been built. God saw that they wanted to do this because of one language which they all spoke. God Almighty again destroys their effort by confusing their language and also by multiplying languages in others, so that they will no longer communicate with each other. Therefore, the people of the world are divided into groups of those who speak the same language among each other, which also leads to different ethnic groups and diversities. Instead of them turning to the Lord and worship; to depend upon him; humanity turned from God to idolatry, sorcery, paganism, worshipping the Moon, the Sun, the mountain, Ocean, and rivers as well engaging in as they discovered astrology. The Spiritual condition of all the people of the Earth was so bad that God gave them up to the sinful desires of their hearts. This was the first time the Lord God visited the earth that he created after the flood. He steps in there and walks around the Tower of Babel and sees the pride of humanity. He went back to heaven but he never stops loving the people of this world that he created in his image, in his likeness.

Chapter Four

The Three Visitors of Abram In Mamre

God turns to Abram to begin the way of salvation for all the people of the world. God remembers his covenant promise that He will not destroy the world anymore. God the Trinity Almighty chose a single single-family again just as he chose Noah. God called a single single-family; to bring redemption to the human race. God the Father, the Son, and the Holy Spirit turned to Abram to begin a way of salvation for all the people of the world. The head of the family was Abram, God changed his name to Abraham.

The Holy Trinity One God forever visited Abram in the City of Mamre; that was the second time Jesus Christ, our Lord made another visit to his people.

The Lord God visited Abraham, which is the fourth Time the Trinitarian God will visit the earth that he created; he called Abram from the land of the Chaldeans before he moved to Haran. God's call to Abram was the motivating factor for (his father) Terah's move to Haran. Abram later became the father of the Jewish nation and many nations today. The Lord appeared and came to the world; this is the third time Jesus Christ, and God, the Father and the Holy Spirit visited the earth according to the Holy Scripture; our Lord and the entire Trinity visited Abraham in the City of Mamre; the Lord made another visit to his people. The three visitors were the Father, the Son, and the Holy Spirit - the Holy Trinity forever one God. The Holy Scripture revealed: "The Lord appeared to Abraham near the great trees of Mamre while he was sitting at the entrance of his tent in the heat of the day. Abraham looked up and saw three men standing nearby. When he saw them, he hurried from the entrance of his tent to meet them and bowed low to the ground. He said, if I have found favor in your eyes, my Lord, do not pass your servant by. Let a little water be brought, and then you may all wash your feet and rest under this tree. Let me get you something to eat, so you can be refreshed and then go on your way -- now that you have come to your servant. Very well, they answered, do as you say. So, Abraham hurried into the tent to Sarah. Quick, he said, get three seahs of fine flour and knead it, and bake some bread. Then he ran to the herd and selected a choice, tender calf, and gave it to a servant, who hurried to prepare it. He then brought some curds, milk and the calf that had been prepared and set them before the three men. While they ate, He stood near them under a tree. Where is your wife, Sarah? They asked him. There, in the tent, he said. Then the Lord said, I will surely return to you about this time next year, and Sarah your wife will have a son. Now Sarah was listening at the entrance of the tent, which was behind him. Abraham and Sarah were already old and well advanced in years, and Sarah was past the age of childbearing. Sarah had already passed the age of childbearing. Sarah laughed to herself as she thought, in her mind, and says: "After I am worn out and my master is old, will I now have this pleasure". Then the Lord said to Abraham, why did Sarah laugh and said, will I have a child, now that I am old? Is anything too hard for the Lord? I will return to you at the appointed time next year and Sarah will have a son. Sarah was afraid, so she lied and said, I did not laugh. But he said, yes, you did laugh."(Genesis 18:1-15) The three visitors were the Father, the Son, and the Holy Spirit. One of the three men was most likely a manifestation of God in human form and the other as angels appearing as men. Abraham may not have initially recognized the visitors as God and angels. They were asking Abraham if there was anything too hard that the Lord cannot do? God Almighty the Father of all mercies, sustainer of all things wants his people to understand that he has the power and love to accomplish what he has promised. Our Lord, Jesus Christ during his earthly ministry emphasizes this truth when he said; with God all things are possible. The essential thing in the calling of Abraham was that God's purpose and his desire that Abraham will be a spiritual leader at home and teach his children the way of the Lord. With the call of Abraham, God established the Father as the head of the family, as the one to be responsible to train his children to keep the way of the Lord by doing what is right and just. We read in the Scripture that: "Now the Lord was gracious to Sarah as he said, and the Lord did for Sarah what he had promised, Sarah becoming pregnant and bore a son to Abraham in his old age, at the very time God had promised him. Abraham gave the name of the baby Isaac to the son Sarah bore him. When his Son Isaac was eight days old, Abraham circumcised him, as God commanded him. Abraham was hundred years old when his son Isaac was born to him. Sarah said, God has brought me laughter and everyone who hears about this will laugh with me. And she added, who would have said, to Abraham that Sara, would nurse children? Yet I have borne him a son in his old age." (Genesis 21:1-7) God Almighty Father always fulfills his promises in our lives from the people in the Old Testament and to the people of the present time. The Father never fails his children, God is an unchangeable God, who always is and always will be forever living. He is the everlasting God. Sarah was pregnant because the Lord opened her womb. God always hears the cry of his children, always hears our prayers, and answers our prayers. Abraham had strong faith in God; he believed in him, he followed his entire commandment and his Word. He was very obedient to the word of God and his Will. Isaac, the promised son was born to Abraham and Sarah. God continues his covenant of the gift of salvation to all the people in the world; God will continue his covenant with Abraham. Twenty-five years passed before the promise of God to Abraham was fulfilled. Our Lord God is good to those whose hope is in him; in his own time, at the appointed time, he will faithfully fulfill his promise just as he said. All glory and honor will be unto him, for whom nothing is impossible to do in the Heaven and on the Earth.

Chapter Five

Who Is Melchizedek?

Jesus Christ is an active agent before the foundation of the world. Jesus Christ is always with the Father; just as he is seated at the right hand of the throne of God the Father right now and reigning in the unity of the Holy Spirit, one God forever and ever. God the Father said it, Jesus Christ carries it out, and the Holy Spirit will empower it. The Holy Scripture reveals: "He is the image of the invisible God, the firstborn over all creation. For in him all things were created: things in heaven and on earth, visible and invisible, whether thrones or powers or rulers or authorities; all things were created by him and for him. He is before all things, and in him all things hold together."(Colossians 1:15-17) Jesus Christ is the firstborn over all creation which implies that Christ Jesus is the incomparable beneficiary; Jesus Christ is the main successor and the leader of all manifestations since he is the everlasting Child.

Through Jesus Christ, everything in paradise and on earth was made. Witness Paul gave a reasonable assertion of the inventive exercises of Jesus Christ before the establishment of the world. All things were made for him, by him, both material and physical, and otherworldly, they owed their reality to Jesus Christ's inventive work as the dynamic specialist in creation. All these hold these holds together and are sustained in Christ Jesus. God Almighty created all things through Jesus Christ. Jesus Christ is the eternal word of God, through him all things were made; without him, nothing was made that has been made; by Christ Jesus, all things were created; visible and invisible; all things were created by him and for him. The book of the Hebrews revealed: "In the past, God spoke to our forefathers through the prophets at many times and in various ways, but in these last days he has spoken to us by his Son, whom he appointed heir of all things, and through whom he made the universe. The Son is the radiance of God's glory and the exact representation of his being, sustaining all things by His powerful Word. After he had provided purification for sin, he sat down at the right hand of the Majesty in heaven. So, he became as much superior to the angels as the name he has inherited is superior to theirs." (Mark 16:19-20)

The Scripture revealed that: "After Abram returned from defeating Chedorlaomer and the kings allied with him, the king of Sodom came out to meet him in the Valley of Shaveh (that is, the King's Valley). Then Melchizedek king of Salem brought out bread and wine. He was a priest of God Most High, and he blessed Abraham, saying, blessed the Abraham by God Most High, Creator of heaven and earth. And blessed be God Most High who delivered your enemies into your hand. Then Abram gave him a tenth of everything. The king of Sodom said to Abram, "Give me the people and keep the goods for yourself. But Abram said to the king of Sodom, I have raised my hand to the Lord, God Most High, Creator of heaven and earth, and have taken an oath that I will accept nothing belonging to you, not even a thread or the thong of a sandal so that you will never be able to say, I made Abram rich. I will accept nothing but what my men have eaten and the share that belongs to the men who went with me -- to Aner, Eshcol, and Mamre, let them have their share."(Genesis 14: 17-24) The Lord appeared and came to the world and lived in the world by the name Melchizedek; the Lord God came to the world the third time through Melchizedek which means King of righteousness, king of Salem, and the priest of God Most High. He served the one true God, like Abram. Melchizedek was probably a Canaanite like Job; he is an example of a godly non-Israelite. Melchizedek is a type, or figure of the royalty and eternal Priesthood of Jesus Christ. The scripture reveals in the book of Psalms: "The Lord has sworn and will not change his mind: You are a Priest forever; in the order of Melchizedek."(Psalm 110:4) We also read in another Scripture, which says: "So Christ also did not take upon himself the glory of becoming a high priest. But God said to him, you are my Son; today I have become your Father. And he says in another place, you are a priest forever in the order of Melchizedek." (Hebrew 5:5-6) Melchizedek was a mysterious Old Testament figure or person who appears in the book of Genesis as God's priest of Salem before the time of the Leviticus priesthood; Christ's priesthood is of the same kind as

Melchizedek. In gratitude for God's help and grace, Abram gave Melchizedek tenth of the spoils he had recovered; which initiated the tithing when it was first mentioned in the Holy Scripture, long before it was commanded by Moses. The Scripture continues: "We have this hope as an anchor for the Soul, firm and secure. It enters the inner sanctuary behind the curtain, where Jesus, who went before us, has entered on our behalf. He has become a high priest forever, in the order of Melchizedek." (Hebrew 6:19-20) In another Scripture: "This Melchizedek was king of Salem and priest of God Most High. He met Abram returning from the defeat of the kings and blessed him, and Abraham gave him a tenth of everything; also, king of Salem means king of peace. Without father or mother, without genealogy, without beginning of days or end of life, like the Son of God, he remains a priest forever. Just think how great he was; even the patriarch Abraham gave him a tenth of the plunder. Now the Law requires the descendants of Levi who become priests to collect a tenth from the people that is, their brothers even though their brothers are descendants from Abraham. This man, however, did not trace his descent from Levi, yet he collected a tenth from Abraham and blessed him who had the promises. And without doubt, the lesser person is blessed by the greater." (Hebrews 7:1-7) Melchizedek was a contemporary of Abraham; he was known as a Canaanite ruler of Salem and a minister of God. Abraham paid an offering to him and was honored by him. He was viewed as a sort of Jesus Christ who both filled in as cleric and ruler; He lived as Canaanites, however he doesn't have a dad or mother, and he was not a relative of Levi and the Leviticus minister. Jesus Christ's brotherhood is in the request for Melchizedek implies that Christ both existed and was more prominent than Abraham. The Sacred text doesn't give us Melchizedek's ancestry and it remains silent with regards to his start and his end. Hence, since the sacred text didn't refer to his start and his end, he fills in as a kind of the everlasting Jesus Christ whose ministry won't ever end. Jesus Christ, without question, is the one that went to the world as Melchizedek, as such, to make it understand that Jesus Christ is Melchizedek, cleric of Most High God, ruler of Salem, lord of Nobility who lives forever more. Jesus Christ is an ideal cleric since he is completely upright, and he gives a change once to all to forfeit for our wrongdoings. He fills in as our timeless minister before God the Father in paradise and lives everlastingly; all who come to God through him are honored with everlasting life.

Chapter Six

Jacob's Vision Of Wrestled With God At Bethel

The Lord God visited the earth and wrestled with Jacob. To know Jacob's story is to realize the crystal clear reality, which he knows that he had a life in which the struggles never ended. Although God promised Jacob that through him would come not only a single great nation but a whole company of nations, however, Jacob, he was a man full of fears and anxieties. At a pivotal point in his life, Jacob was about to meet his brother, Esau, who had vowed to kill him. It was going to be a turning point for his destiny as all Jacob's struggles and fears were about to be realized. Sick of his father-in-law's treatment, Jacob had fled Laban, only to encounter his embittered brother, Esau. Anxious and fearful for his very life, Jacob concocted a bribe and sent a caravan of gifts along with his women and children across the River Jabbok in hopes of pacifying his brother. Now physically exhausted, alone in the desert wilderness, facing inevitable death, he was divested of all his worldly possessions. He was powerless to control his faith and felt weak. He collapsed into a deep sleep on the banks of the Jabbok River. With his father-in-law behind him and Esau before him, he was too exhausted to struggle any longer.

The Scripture reveals: "That night Jacob got up and took his two wives, his two maidservants, and his eleven sons and crossed the ford of the Jabbok. After he had sent them across the stream, he sent over all his possessions. So Jacob was left alone, and a man wrestled with him till daybreak, but Jacob replied I will not let you go unless you bless me. The man asked him, What is your name? "Jacob", he answered. Then the man said, your name will no longer be Jacob, but Israel because you have struggled with God and with men and have overcome. Jacob said, please tell me your name. But he replied, why do you ask my name? Then he blessed him there. So Jacob called the place Peniel, saying It is because I saw God face to face, and yet my life was spared. The sun rose above him as he passed Peniel, and he was limping because of his hip. Therefore to this day, the Israelites do not eat the tendon attached to the socket of the hip, because the socket of Jacob's hip was touched near the tendon." (Genesis 32: 22-32) NIV

The man who wrestled with Jacob and called himself the angel of the Lord, might be Jesus Christ Himself. He who is identified with God himself or the Son of God. Since Jacob wrestled desperately for the promise and blessings he intended to earn, God allowed him to prevail. Yet as a reminder that Jacob must rely on God entirely and not walk the Earth with his own strength, God disabled Jacob's hip. It was a reminder that Jacob must no longer walk in his strength but walk in dependence on God.

The name of Jacob, which implied a crafty deceiver, was now changed to Israel, which means, 'he struggles with God'. All believing Christians, especially those who follow Jesus Christ faithfully, are sometimes called the Israel of God. God Almighty Father does not want His people to be passive but to earnestly seek Him for His blessings and His grace. God Almighty blessed Jacob on the night of his Fight with Him, which also is a proof of God's blessing on Jacob's life.

From there onwards, Jacob knew that his life and his well-being were dependent not on his own devices but on the help of God, His guidance, and His blessing. Later, God reminded the descendants of Jacob, Israel of this truth when He said: "Not by might nor power, but by my Spirit, says the Lord Almighty." (Zechariah 4:6) NIV

These words of God the Father, God the Son, and God the Holy Spirit Forever One God Holy Trinity apply to all believing Christians that walk on this Earth. It reminds us that we can only do the work of the Lord when the power of the Holy Spirit operates in our lives. Jesus Christ entered and started his earthly ministry in the power of the Spirit of God. The church was empowered by the Holy Spirit on the day of Pentecost; before then, they were all hidden inside the upper room in Jerusalem, terrified to come outside. Only with an incessant flow of the Power and presence of the Spirit of God in our lives can we be able to serve Him faithfully and truthfully.

The People of God and all the Christian Believers earn victory and blessings from God in the same way. The cycle never ceases. While we may not wrestle physically with God, we can seek Him earnestly and persistently in our prayers. We must confess our sins and ask Him for forgiveness. We must have the hunger and thirst for His kingdom. We should constantly seek an intimate relationship with Him and His full presence. We must desire the reality and power of the Holy Spirit and as well as pursue a life of true holiness, faith, and righteousness. Our Lord and Savior the Son of God and the Son of man, came down from heaven and blessed Jacob after he tested his faith and truthfulness to God by wrestling with Him till daybreak. He changed Jacob's name and blessed him, God Almighty is still doing the same even till today.

Up till today, If you are in Christ, you are the seed of Abraham, Isaac, and Jacob which means whatever you might be going through affliction, rejection, tribulations, persecutions; but you are not alone, and the reward is great. We have been given the rights of possession and the authority to rule what we possess. It has always been God's plan for mankind, for humanity to have dominion over the earth, which will not fail. The Scripture reveals: "God blessed them and said to them, be fruitful and increase in number, fill the earth and subdue it. Rule over the fish of the sea and the birds of the air and over every living creature that moved on the ground."(Genesis 1:28) NIV.

Christian believers must have a strong faith in the Lord and continue to strengthen and grow in their faith. They should focus their heart and minds on Jesus Christ, the mediator, author, and finisher of our faith. It is the reward of all the faithful Christian believers who operate their lives with uttered Gospel words as well as , unshakable faith; they will receive the promises of God.

We are the children of God in Christ Jesus; therefore, we must show patience over the things we desire. There are so many things that concern us, but we need to stop asking God to give us all. Instead, we must just start thanking Him for giving us all we needed for life and liberty. What God gave us; is ours from this earth to heaven, belongs to us. No one has the power to take it from us. Abraham believed in God's promise, and God accounted it to him for his righteousness. Our Lord Jesus Christ said, "If you believe, all things are possible for those who believe." (Mark 9:23) NIV.

Chapter Seven

The Fourth Person in The Furnace With Shadrach, Meshach, And Abednego

God the Father, Son, and Holy Spirit never leaves His people. He visited the Earth that He created to glorify His Holy name, exhibit His power, and extend His grace in every area of our lives in great detail. He never lets His believers suffer affliction, trial, and persecution. They may go through these sufferings, but the Lord is always there to take care of them. The Scripture revealed in the book of Daniels: "King Nebuchadnezzar made an image of gold, ninety feet high and nine feet wide, and set it up on the plain of Dura in the province of Babylon. He then summoned the satraps, prefects, governors, advisers, treasurers, judges, magistrates, and all the other provincial officials to come to the dedication of the image he had set up. So, the Satraps, treasurers, judges, magistrates, and all the other provincial officials assembled for the dedication of the image that King

Nebuchadnezzar had set up, and they stood before it."(Daniel 3:1-3)

Nebuchadnezzar carried out this proud act because of his dream. Nebuchadnezzar's empire had just risen to power. He was undoubtedly trying to use religion to consolidate the many provinces he had added to his empire. He demanded people to worship the image and considered the act as loyalty to him. He was not the first, nor will he be the last world leader who tried to use religion for political purposes or self-exaltation.

The Scripture continued and revealed: "Therefore, as soon as they heard the sound of the horn, flute, zither, lyre, harp and all kinds of music, all the people, nations and men of every language fell and worshipped the image of gold that King Nebuchadnezzar had set up. At this time, some astrologers came forward and denounced the Jews. They said to King Nebuchadnezzar, 'O King, live forever! You have issued a decree, O King, that everyone who hears the sound of the horn, flute, zither, lyre, harp, pipes, and all kinds of music must fall and worship the image of gold, and whoever does not fall and worship will be thrown into the blazing furnace. But there are some Jews whom you have set over the affairs of the province of Babylon - Shadrach, Meshach, and Abednego who pay no attention to you, O King. They neither serve your gods nor worship the image of gold you have set up.' The King was furious. Nebuchadnezzar summoned Shadrach, Meshach, and Abednego, so these men were brought before the King. And Nebuchadnezzar said to them, 'Is it true, Shadrach, Meshach, and Abednego, that you do not serve my gods or worship the image of gold I have set up? Now, when you hear the sound of the horn, flute, zither, lyre, harp pipes, and all kinds of music, if you are ready to fall and worship the image, I made, very good. But if you do not worship it, you will be thrown immediately into a blazing furnace. Then what god will be able to rescue you from my hand?' Shadrach, Meshach, and Abednego replied to the King, 'O Nebuchadnezzar, we do not need to defend ourselves before you in this matter if we are thrown into the blazing furnace, the God we serve can save us from your hand, O King. But even if he does not, we want you to know, O King, that we will not serve your gods or worship the image of gold you have set up. Then Nebuchadnezzar was furious with Shadrach, Meshach, and Abednego, and his attitude towards them changed. He ordered the furnace heated seven times hotter than usual and commanded some of the strongest soldiers in his army to tie up Shadrach, Meshach, and Abednego and throw them into the blazing furnace. So, these men, wearing their robes, trousers, turbans, and other clothes, were bound and thrown into the blazing furnace.

The King's command was so urgent and the furnace so hot that the flames of the fire killed the soldiers who took up Shadrach, Meshach, and Abednego, and these three men, firmly tied, fell into the blazing furnace. Then King Nebuchadnezzar leapt to his feet in amazement and asked his advisers, weren't there three men that we tied up and threw into the fire?

They replied, 'Certainly, O king.' He said, 'Look, I see four men walking around in the fire, unbound and unharmed, and the fourth looks like a son of the gods.' Nebuchadnezzar then approached the opening of the blazing furnace and shouted, 'Shadrach, Meshach, and Abednego, servant of the Most High God, come out, come here!' So, Shadrach, Meshach, and Abednego came out of the fire, and the satraps, prefects, governors, and royal advisers crowded around them. They saw that the fire had not harmed their bodies, nor was a hair of their heads singed; their robes were not scorched, and there was no smell of fire on them. Then Nebuchadnezzar said, 'Praise be to the God of Shadrach, Meshach, and Abednego, who has sent his Angel and rescued his servants! They trusted in him, defied the King's command, and were willing to give up their lives rather than serve or worship any god except their own God. Therefore, I decree that the people of any nation or language who say anything against the God of Shadrach, Meshach, and Abednego be cut into pieces, and their houses be turned into piles of rubble, for no other God can save in this way.' Then the King promoted Shadrach, Meshach, and Abednego in the province of Babylon."(Daniel 3: 7-30)

Nebuchadnezzar was very proud of the image of gold that he had put together for his people to worship as their God. He ordered them to bow down to the image of the gold statue. He had just risen into power, and he was trying to exercise his power over all the provinces that he added to his empire; therefore, he demanded the worship of the people instead of worshipping the Creator of heaven and Earth. Until today, whenever people get into power, they always forget about God Almighty, who created them in His image, especially in a political system. They like to control people's spiritual life. They want to manipulate people's faith in the God they believe in and worship. During the Israelites exile in Babylon, Daniel's three friends Shadrach, Meshach, and Abednego, were appointed by the King. They were given the responsibility in Babylonian administration, while Daniel served in the King's court. People of God must not under any circumstances worship or give divine honor to any fake god or any image or statue representing a god or goddess. The King's command was so urgent and frightening to all the people. Yet these three young men stood by their word and did not hesitate in showing their allegiance to the one true God. They had hope for strength; moreover, they knew that God's wrath against sin and disobedience was worse than any wrath a human can impose on them. Therefore, their determination was an expression of unconditional faith. They had complete trust in God and total loyalty towards Him from their core. They possessed a religion that was powerful enough to trust and obey God, regardless of the consequences. The actual evidence of the true biblical faith lies in the obedience and concrete trust in God regardless of the experience of deliverance. God has given us examples of so many people like these in the Holy Bible. Shadrach, Meshach, and Abednego demonstrated their great faith in God when tested, and they earned the victory for the Lord.

The fourth person in the blazing furnace was the Son of God, Jesus Christ, who came down to protect them. He was the pre-incarnate manifestation of Christ and came to be with them in their time of great trial. He showed His grace and mercy to them and helped them. The Lord came down and was with them inside the blazing furnace because Shadrach, Meshach, and Abednego remained true to God even at the possible cost of their lives.

All Christian adherents ought to be steady in their supplications that God All-powerful assists them in all walks of Life. He strengthens us by putting a firm assurance inside our souls and minds to stay consistent with Him and His assertion without being afraid of the natural results. Lord Nebuchadnezzar acknowledged and vouched for God's significance, benevolence, love, and power.

Chapter Eight

The Trinity: The Word In Human Form In The Manger

Jesus Christ and the entire Trinity visited the world and stayed longer than ever before. The Scripture reveals that the Trinitarian God continues to make this world a better place to live. He spoke through the prophets. He made himself known again and again through his words. Then He decided to send his Son whom He had ordained before the foundation of the world. The Scripture revealed: "In the sixth month, God sent the angel Gabriel to Nazareth, a town in Galilee, to a virgin pledged to be married to a man named Joseph, a descendant of David. The virgin's name was Mary. The angel went to her and said, Greetings, you who are highly favored! The Lord is with you. Mary was greatly troubled at his words and wondered what kind of greeting this might be. But the angel said to her, do not be afraid, Mary, you have found favor with God. You will be with a child and give birth to a son, and you are to give him the name Jesus. He will be great and will be called the Son of Most High. The Lord God will give him the throne of his father David, and he will reign over the house of Jacob forever; his kingdom will never end. How will this be, Mary asked the angel, since I am a virgin? The angel answered, The Holy Spirit will come upon you, and the power of the Most High will overshadow you. So the holy one to be born will be called the Son of God. Even Elizabeth, your relative, is going to have a child in her old age, and she who was said to be barren is in her sixth month. For nothing is impossible with God." (Luke 1:26-37)

The Lord Almighty Father, the Holy Trinity forever one God was planning the redemptive work of Jesus Christ; and to execute it. He sent angel Gabriel to Virgin Mary who was favored above all the women in the world then and now, and she will continue to be till the end of the age among all women. Virgin Mary was chosen as the mother of Jesus. We must remember that Virgin Mary merits our utter respect, but she is not to be worshipped as God or referred to as the mother of God. As the true believers of the Lord, only Jesus Christ merits our worship. Mary was chosen because she found favor with God the Father, the Son, and the Holy Spirit. Her humility and her godly life pleased God to such an extent that He chose her for this most sacred and significant task.

The Power of the Holy Spirit came upon Mary, and by a miraculous act of God Almighty, the child was conceived without sexual intercourse. It is the ultimate proof for the world that Jesus Christ is holy and sinless. Mary submitted herself completely to the will of God and trusted in angel Gabriel's message. She willingly accepted the honor. She accepted the reproach that comes with being the mother of the holy child; she observed complete faith in God and His Word and had a devoted heart to obey the Holy Spirit.

Mary recognized her own need for salvation; she was also a sinner in need of a Savior. Jesus Christ is the manifold wisdom of God. He is the perfect revelation of the nature and person of God. Jesus Christ is the utter reflection of God's word and thus reveals the heart and mind of God Himself. Apostle John gives us a clear picture of how Jesus Christ is the Word of God. The book also describes the three main characteristics of Jesus as the Word. The Holy Scripture says in the gospel of John: "In the beginning was the word, and the word, was with God, and the Word was God. He was with God in the beginning. Through him, all things was made; without him, nothing was made that has been made. In him was life, and that life was the light of men. The light shines in the darkness, but the darkness has not understood it." (John 1:1-5) Apostle John began his gospel by calling Jesus Christ the Word of God, "The Word." Jesus Christ is the personal Word of God. God spoke His Word into Virgin Mary's womb just as He spoke the earth into existence by saying, "Let there be light, and it was light."

God transferred His Son into Mary's womb and His Word transformed into flesh. Jesus Christ dwelled among us for thirty-three glorious years on the Earth – the Earth that he created. Jesus Christ is the manifold wisdom of God. He is the only and the perfect revelation of nature of God, for He is the person of God. Jesus Christ as the Word of God reveals the heart and mind of God to us. Apostle John gives us a clear picture of how Jesus Christ is the Word of God; he mentions three main characteristics of Jesus as the Word. Jesus Christ is the Word of God concerning God the Father.

Christ Jesus existed with God before the creation of the universe. Christ as a person existed from eternity, distinct from the world, but He was always in an eternal fellowship with God the Father. Jesus Christ is divine; He is God. He is the Son of God and has the same nature and essence as God the Father. Jesus Christ came into the world as the Word of God. Through Jesus Christ, God the Father created the world, and He will remain to be the reason that God sustains the world even now.

The Son of God took our image and our likeness. He adapted the human nature without touching any impurity of any kind of sin and lived among us. Jesus Christ, the incarnate Son of God, left heaven and transformed into human form through human birth.

He left all his glory in heaven and came down to this world of sin to save the sinners and the ones who were lost in darkness. Jesus Christ was the light of men; genuine life is embodied in the existence of Jesus Christ. Every human being on Earth has lived a life under the life of Jesus Christ. God's truth, nature, and power are made available to all people through Jesus Christ, the Savior and the Lord of all the people on earth. The light of Jesus Christ works as a blessing in this sinful and evil world that is being controlled by Satan. I will continue to be like this until all the people in the world are evangelized by moving from darkness to Christ's marvelous light. Jesus Christ illumines all who hear the gospel by imparting a measure of grace and understanding on them so that they may freely choose to accept or reject the gospel message of salvation. Apart from Jesus Christ's light, there is no other light by which humanity may see the truth and be saved. The world and the people of this world did not recognize Jesus Christ, especially those who were the enemy and the haters of God and the Cross of Christ.

Another Scripture says: "For God so loved the world that he gave his one and only Son, that whoever believes in him shall not perish but have eternal life. For God did not send his Son into the world to condemn the world, but to save the world through him. Whoever believes in him is not condemned but whoever does not believe stands condemned already because he has not believed in the name of God's one and only Son. This is the verdict: Light has come into the world, but men loved darkness instead of light because their deeds were evil." (John 3:16-19)

God loves this world so much, and He wants everyone to be saved God's love is wide enough to embrace all the people on earth. God gave His only incarnate begotten Son as an offering for our sins on the cross. The atonement proceeded from the loving heart of God. It was not something forced on Him. The Father planned it, the Son carried it out, and the Holy Spirit empowered it. The Scripture says in the book of Hebrews: "In the past, God spoke to our forefathers through the prophets at many times and in various ways. But in these last days, he has spoken to us by his Son whom he appointed heir of all things, and through whom he made the universe. The Son is the radiance of God's glory and the exact representation of his being, sustaining all things by His powerful word. After he had provided purification for sins, he sat down at the right hand of the Majesty in heaven." (Hebrew 1: 1-3)

Chapter Nine

He Who Created The Animals Came To Them First In The Manger

The birth of Jesus Christ is described in these words in the Holy Scripture: "So Joseph also went up from the town of Nazareth in Galilee to Judea, to Bethlehem the town of David, because he belonged to the house and line of David. He went there to register with Mary, who was pledged to be married to him and was expecting a child. While they were there, the time came for the baby to be born, and she gave birth to her firstborn, a Son. She wrapped him in cloths and placed him in a manger because there was no room for them in the inn. And shepherds were living out in the fields nearby, keeping watch over their flocks at night. An angel of the Lord appeared to them, and the glory of the Lord shone around them, and they were terrified. But the angel said to them, do not be afraid. I bring you good news of great joy that will be for all the people. Today in the town of

David, a Savior has been born to you; he is Christ the Lord. This will be a sign to you: You will find a baby wrapped in clothes and lying in a manger. Suddenly a great company of the heavenly host appeared with the angel, praising God and saying, Glory to God in the highest, and on earth peace to men on whom his favor rests. When the angels had left them and gone into heaven, the shepherds said to one another. Let's go to Bethlehem and see this thing that has happened, which the Lord has told us about. So they hurried off and found Mary and Joseph, and the baby, who was lying in the manger. The shepherds returned, glorifying and praising God for all the things they had heard and seen, which were just as they had been told." (Luke 2:4-16,20)

At the beginning of creation, God made the creatures first and later made Adam and Eve. God ensured that whatever He has created was acceptable, and that is how He favored them. When God went to the Nursery of Eden and took a walk with Adam and Eve, the livestock and all the other creatures were available.

Just like when He converted Himself in the human structure, He also transformed Himself in all the animals and creatures sent into the world for the first time. God did it to keep reminding us that He stayed with all the creations that He had made.

Similarly, Christ Jesus was brought into the world in a trough in every one of the creatures and birds; it was not a slip-up; it was to tell them that he is the Lord, all things considered. Jesus Christ was brought into the world in a Stable, where creatures were kept. The stable was likely a cavern and the trough a feeder for creatures.

The birth of the Savior, the greatest event in the history of this universe, occurred in the humblest of circumstances. Jesus Christ is undoubtedly the King of Kings, but He was neither born as a King nor glorified in the King's palace, and nor did He live like a King in this world. Through his example, we can believe that all the people of God, the believing Christians, are actual kings and priests in eternal life, but in this world, we must be as humble and simple as Jesus Christ was.

Upon Jesus Christ's birth, He was called a Savior. As a Savior, He came to deliver us the message of God. He shed His light on an ungodly world of fear, death, and sins, dominated by Satan's power – it was the condemnation of our transgressions. The Savior is also Christ Jesus our Lord. He has been anointed as the Messiah of God and the Lord who rules over His people. None can have Jesus Christ as a Savior if they do not submit to His Lordship. The Holy Scripture also revealed that the Magi also visited Jesus when He was born: "After Jesus was born in Bethlehem in Judea, during the time of King Herod, Magi from the east came to Jerusalem and asked, where is the one who has been born King of the Jews? We saw his star in the east and have come to worship him. When King Herod heard this, he was disturbed, and all Jerusalem with him. When he had called together all the people's chief priests and teachers of the law, he asked them where Christ was to be born. In Bethlehem in Judea, they replied, for this is what the prophet has written. After they had heard the king, they went on their way, and the star they had seen in the east went ahead of them until it stopped over the place where the child was. When they saw the star, they were overjoyed. On coming to the house, they saw the child with his mother Mary, and they bowed down and worshiped him. Then they opened their treasures and presented him with gifts of gold and incense, and myrrh. And having been warned in a dream not to go back to Herod, they returned to their country by another route." (Matthew 2:1-5,9-12)

Prophet Isaiah prophesied the birth of Jesus Christ the Lord: "Therefore the Lord himself will give you a sign: The Virgin will be with child and will give birth to a son, and will call him Emmanuel." (Isaiah 7:14) Prophet Isaiah prophesied the birth of Jesus; the immediate application of this sign was to a new bride who would have been a virgin until the time of her marriage. Virgin Mary realized this prophecy's fulfillment during the birth of Jesus Christ. Mary, who was a virgin and remained a virgin until after the divine child was born, became the medium of a miracle birth. The conception was made possible by the miracle of the Holy Spirit instead of through the act of a man.

The Son was called Emmanuel God with us, God in us. The Lord came down from heaven as a baby in the manger. The value of the Virgin's birth cannot be over-emphasized. For Christ, our redeemer, to be qualified to pay for our sins and bring salvation to the world, He must be in one person, fully human, sinless, and fully divine. The virgin birth satisfies all three of these requirements: (1) The only way Jesus Christ could be born a human being was to be born from the womb of a woman. (2) The only way Christ Jesus could be sinless was to be conceived by the Holy Spirit. (3) The only way Jesus Christ could be divine was to have God as His father.

As a result, the conception of Jesus Christ was not natural but supernatural, which means the Holy One to be born will be called the Son of God. Jesus Christ is, therefore, revealed: To us as one divine person with two natures; the divine and the sinless human being. Jesus Christ lived in our world and suffered as a human. Jesus Christ sympathized with our weaknesses. As the divine Son of God, He has the power to deliver us from sin's bondage and Satan's power. Jesus Christ was conceived by the Holy Spirit without the intervention of a human father and was given birth by Mary, who was still a virgin. Christ Jesus is divine and as human, He qualifies to serve as a sacrifice for the sins of all the people. Also, He has the right in every ways to be the High Priest to intercede for all who come to God through Him. Jesus as a Savior will save His people from their sins because sin is the greatest enemy of the human being, destroying one's soul and life. Through the atoning death of Jesus Christ and the sanctifying power of the Holy Spirit, those who turn to Christ Jesus will be set free from guilt and slavery of sin. The Scripture continues: "On the eighth day when it was time to circumcise him, he was named Jesus, the name that the angel had given him before he had been conceived. When the time of their purification according to the Law of Moses had been completed, Joseph and Mary took him to Jerusalem to present him to the Lord; as it is written in the Law of the Lord, every firstborn male is to be consecrated to the Lord, and to offer a sacrifice in keeping with what is said in the Law of the Lord; a pair of doves or two young pigeons. Now there was a man in Jerusalem called Simeon, who was righteous and devout. He was waiting for the consolation of Israel, and the Holy Spirit was upon him. It had been revealed to him by the Holy Spirit that he would not die before he had seen the Lord's Christ. Moved by the Spirit, he went into the temple courts. When the parents brought in the child Jesus to do for him what the custom of the Law required, Simeon took him in his arms and praised God. The child's father and mother marveled at what was said about him. Then Simeon blessed them and said to Mary, his mother, this child is destined to cause the falling and rising of many in Israel and to be a sign that will be spoken against so that the thoughts of many hearts will be revealed. And a sword will pierce your soul too. There was also a prophetess, Anna, the daughter of Phanuel, of the tribe of Asher. She was very old; she had lived with her husband seven years after her marriage and then was a widow until she was eighty-four. She never left the temple but worshiped night and day, fasting and praying. Coming up to them at that very moment, she gave thanks to God and spoke about the child to all who were looking forward to the redemption of Jerusalem. When Joseph and Mary had done everything required by the Law of the Lord, they returned to Galilee to their town of Nazareth."(Luke 2:21-28; 33-39)

Joseph and Mary presented Jesus Christ to the Lord so that all Christian parents should sincerely consecrate their children to the Lord. They should constantly pray every day for their children's life, from the beginning to the end, to follow the path of God. May they have the unshakable faith and will to serve and glorify God with complete devotion to our Lord.

Savior Jesus Christ was identified with the poor and underprivileged right from his birth in the manger. Simeon was devoted and righteous in the sight of God. He was filled with the power of the Holy Spirit. He waited with faith, patience, and a great longing for the arrival of the Messiah. Just as, we are waiting for the return of our Lord today. Some people might lose hope and fall off, but there will always be many faithful ones like Simeon who will wait for the arrival of the Lord. Our greatest blessing is to see the Lord Jesus Christ face to face and be ready when He comes. We will live with Him forever in His presence.

Same was the case with Anna, who worshiped day and night; she was constantly fasting and praying. Anna was a prophetess who earnestly hoped for the coming of Jesus Christ. For many years, she remained a widow, never remarrying but devoted herself to the Lord.

Chapter Ten

Jesus Christ Growing Up In Nazareth

The Holy Scripture continues with the stories of Jesus Christ when he was just a boy, growing up in Nazareth with His earthly parent. The boy Jesus, who was lost and found in the temple after three days:

"Every year, His parents went to Jerusalem for the Feast of the Passover. When he was twelve years old, they went up to the Feast, according to the custom. After the Feast was over, while His parents were returning home, the boy Jesus stayed behind in Jerusalem, but they were unaware of it. Thinking he was in their company, they traveled on for a day. Then they began looking for Him among their relatives and friends. When they did not find Him, they went back to Jerusalem to look for Him. After three days, they found him in the temple courts, sitting among the teachers listening to them and asking them questions. Everyone who heard Him was amazed at his understanding and His answers. When his parents saw Him, they were astonished. His mother said to Him, Son, why have you treated us like this? Your father and I have been anxiously searching for you. Why were you searching for me? He asked. Didn't you know I had to be at my Father's house? But they did not understand what He was saying to them. Then He went down to Nazareth with them and was obedient to them. But his mother treasured all these things in her heart. And Jesus grew in wisdom and stature, and in favor with God and men." (Luke 2:41-52)

Jesus Christ as a true human child, experienced the process of physical and spiritual development. He kept increasing in wisdom as the grace of God was upon him. He was perfect in His human nature, developing perfectly as God desired Him to be.

Jesus Christ grew with great wisdom. After what happened at the temple at the age of twelve, Christ spent his life without any problem with his parents or with anyone for good eighteen years.

What did his life look like during those eighteen years before He started His full ministry? Jesus Christ used to sit with the teachers of the Law, asking questions and answering questions when He was only twelve years old. He told them that he was a divine teacher, but he humbled himself among them in human form.

He wanted to start His work before the time, but the Holy Spirit corrected him and put Him in subjection to his parents. We learn that He grew up in a large family. His father was a carpenter, and that is how Jesus learned the trade from His father. Since Joseph is never mentioned again in the gospel, it is likely that Joseph died before Jesus Christ began his public ministry. It is also likely that Jesus provided for His mother and His younger brothers and sisters.

Jesus worked as a Carpenter, mastering all the skills like household repairs, furniture-making, and construction of agricultural implements, such as plows and yokes. According to the Will, Christ grew and developed physically and spiritually during those years and was fully conscious that God was His Father. Jesus Christ's love and obedience to the Father and the Holy Spirit are incomparable. Jesus Christ was baptized according to the Holy Scripture as He continued to live among the people on the earth he created.

The Scripture revealed: "Now when all the people were being baptized, Jesus was baptized too. And as he was praying, the heaven was opened, and the Holy Spirit descended upon him in bodily form like a dove. And a voice came from heaven: You are my Son, the Beloved; with you, I am well pleased. Now Jesus himself was about thirty years old when he began his ministry. He was the Son (as was thought) of Joseph, the son of Heli." (Luke 3:21-23)

These are the ancestors of Jesus Christ from Joseph the earthly father of Jesus Christ according to the Scripture: "Joseph the son of Heli, Son of Matthat, son of Levi, son of Melchi, son of Jannai, son of Joseph, son of Mattathias, son of Amos, son of Nahum. Son of Esli, son of Naggai, son of Maath, son of Mattathias, son of Semein, son of Joseph, son of Joda, son of Joanan, son of Rhesa, son of Zerubbabel, son of Shealtiel, son of Neri, son of Melchi, son of Addi, son of Cosam, son of Elmadam, son of Er, son of Joshua, son of Eliezer, son of Jorim, son of Matthat, son of Levi, son of Simmon, son of Judah, son of Joseph, son of Jonam, son of Eliakim, son of Melea, son of Menna, son of Mattatha, son og Nathan, son of David, son of Jesse, son of Obed, son of Boaz, son of Sala, son of Nahshon, son of Amminadab, son of Admin, son of Armi, son of Hezron, son of Perez, son of of Judah, son of Jacob, son of Isaac, son of Abraham, son of Terah, son of Nahor, son of Serug, son of Reu, son of Peleg, son og Eber, son os Shelah, son of Cainan, son of Arphaxed, son of Shem, son of Noah, son of lamech, son of Methuselah, son of Enoch, son of Jared, son of Mahalaleed, son of Cainan, son of Enos, son of Seth, son of Adam, son of God" (Luke 3: 23-38)

The gospel of Matthew traced Jesus Christ's roots back to Abraham, father of the Jewish people and race. But the gospel of Luke , being the only Gentle writer of the New Testament, emphasized that Jesus' good news was for all the people in the whole wide world; not just the Jews alone. In keeping with that purpose in our mind, he carried and completed Jesus Christ's lineage all the way back to the first man on earth, Adam.

Chapter Eleven

Christ Jesus Tempted By Satan As Adam And Eve Was Tempted In The Garden Of Eden

Christ Jesus, our Lord and Savior, was baptized at the age of thirty years old, and the Holy Spirit descended upon him. Jesus Christ was conceived and in-dwelt by the Holy Spirit from the beginning. Then, he was personally anointed and empowered by the Spirit for the work of the ministry. Jesus Christ was empowered by the Holy Spirit. Jesus was tested by Satan's temptation; since then, the Father planned it, the Son carried it out, and the Holy Spirit empowered it. Father, Son, and the Holy Spirit forever one God.

The Scripture revealed: "Jesus, full of the Holy Spirit, returned from the Jordan and was led by the Spirit in the desert, where for forty days he was tempted by the devil. He ate nothing during those days, and at the end of them, he was hungry. The devil said to him, if you are the Son of God, tell this stone to become bread. Jesus answered, it is written: Man does not live on bread alone. The devil led him up to a high place and showed him in an instant all the kingdoms of the world. And said to him, I will give you all their authority and splendor, for it has been given to me, and I can give it to anyone I want to. So, if you worship me, it will all be yours. Jesus answered, It is written: worship the Lord your God and serve him only. The devil led him to Jerusalem and had him stand on the highest point of the temple. If you are the Son of God, he said, throw yourself down from here. For it is written: He will command his angels concerning you to guard you carefully; they will lift you in their hands so that you will not strike your foot against a stone. Jesus answered. It says: Do not put the Lord your God to the test. When the devil had finished all this tempting, he left him until an opportune time. Jesus returned to Galilee in the power of the Spirit, and news about him spread through the whole countryside. He taught in their synagogues, and everyone praised him." (Luke 4:1-15)

Before Jesus Christ began His natural service,

he was enticed by Satan. One significant and fundamental element of Jesus' enticement rotated around: What sort of Savior He will be and how will He utilize the blessings of God? Jesus Christ was lured to utilize His blessing and position to serve Satan's plan. Satan wanted Jesus to achieve brilliance and control over the countries that resist the cross and the method of affliction. He wanted Jesus to choose a version (as per individuals' well-known assumption) that suits a political Savior.

Satan entices Christian pioneers to utilize the blessing, position, and capacity given to them to fulfill their responsibility to set up their magnificence and realm and to focus on individuals instead of God. The people who compromise with Satan, in all actuality, give Him the ground to control. This way, these people lose the power that comes from breezing through the assessment when enticed. Jesus Christ breezed through the assessment and emerged from the desert with power and control over fiendish spirits and all types of disorder. Christ Jesus defeated every one of Satan's allurements effectively by proclaiming the will and expression of God no matter how much Satan tried to convince him. Jesus Christ remained persistent in his beliefs; he believed that all that is significant in life relies upon God and his Will.

If one reaches for progress, joy, or materialistic things while ignoring the method of God, then by God's will, an unpleasant dissatisfaction that fizzles will be prompted in the person's life. Our Master Jesus Christ accentuated this reality when He instructed that before anything in life, we should first look for the realm of God and his honorableness. We must seek God's standard, the action of God, and the His Force in our lives. If we follow His command and His lead, everything else would be provided to us automatically. Any remaining essential things will be given to us as indicated by His will and way.

Satan tempted Christ Jesus with the offer of dominion over all the kingdoms of the world. Christ refused to seek a kingdom for Himself by bowing down to the worldly methods of compromise, earthly power, political maneuvering, external violence, popularity, honor, and glory. Jesus' kingdom is a spiritual kingdom where He rules in the hearts of His people. These are the people who have been taken out of the kingdoms of the world. As loyal subjects of the heavenly kingdom, we are to be characterized by the fruit of the Holy Spirit's meekness and humility. We must possess the willingness to suffer for righteousness' sake. All believing Christians must give their bodies as a living and holy sacrifice in complete devotion, love, worship, and obedience to God Almighty Father. We must put our trust in spiritual weapons in our war against sin, Satan, and temptation.

Most importantly, we have to stay persistent in resisting or conforming to the patterns of this sinful world. We must be able to stay in the word of God and rebuke any Satan's temptation just as our Lord Jesus Christ did. We must focus on the will of God and things of heaven and pray without ceasing to defeat the enemy with the power of the Holy Spirit. All believing Christians on Earth must ask for the power of the Holy Spirit – the strength to be able to live a complete Christian life. We should pray every day to serve the Lord in any area of the ministry that He assigns to us to do for Him and praise His Glory every day of our lives.

Chapter Twelve

Jesus Christ's Ministry of Reconciliation Begins

The Hebrew Scriptures' sacred texts are loaded with accounts of how God's disclosure and prophetic Word came in many parts. It explains to us the numerous approaches of God to the individuals, the complete of which was uncovered in the Hebrew Scriptures; yet, it didn't amount to the completion of what God needed to say. In any case, for now and forever, God has uncovered Himself to us through his child Jesus Christ. Jesus Christ is incomparable over all things; God's statement through Him is full, last, complete, and rises above every one of the past expressions of God. No one is equal to Him – neither the prophets nor the heavenly messengers. However, Moses has authority equivalent to Jesus', the Child of God. Christ is the main wellspring of everlasting salvation as He serves as the main middle person between God and people. Christ's matchless quality has been affirmed through numerous extraordinary disclosures about Him as God the Child. After giving the pardoning of our wrongdoings by His demise on the cross, Jesus Christ took his spot of power at God's right hand. Christ's reclaiming action in paradise includes his service as a heavenly middle person, go-between, and Baptizer of the Essence of God.

Since Jesus Christ is better than the prophets and the heavenly messengers, even in his child form, there can be no question about his sacredness.

Holy messengers assumed a significant part in giving the Hebrew Scriptures pledge. Jesus Christ as the Child of God emanates the greatness of God since He shares God's tendency and pith. Whatever God is in his person and in His nature, Jesus is His exact portrayal. Thusly, the disclosure of God is, at this point, not fragmentary and inadequate as portrayed in the Hebrew Scriptures times. In Jesus Christ, the Child, the disclosure of the Dad is presently finished for all eternity.

Jesus Christ is the revealer of God and the

reconciler of God; through Him, we got the pardoning of our wrongdoing, the restoration of the body, and life never-ending. He accommodated us to God with the goal that we can call God Abba – our Father in paradise. Jesus Christ, the Baptizer of the Essence of God, has given us a better purpose, a

more noteworthy longing, and an ability to witness the saving work of the Ruler Jesus Christ. We will want to get direction cognizance and the assistance of the Master. We will want to have the full presence of the Essence of God in our everyday lives. After completing the Essence of God, we will want to feel the Soul's Force, His full presence, heading, directing, and prompting the method of uprightness. Most importantly, we will want to see the soul winning in the hands of the Master Jesus Christ.

Surprisingly, the Essence of God wanted salvation on the planet since God, the Father Child the Essence of God, needs everybody to be saved. He didn't want anybody to die however, the information appeal to God for the pardoning that is just in Christ Jesus our Savior.

All the trusting Christians brought back to life in this universe should keep a genuine conviction with God. They must stand firm in their belief that Jesus Christ is the genuine Child of God and the main Guardian Angel for the lost mankind. Likewise, they should have a self-giving partnership with dutifulness to the Master Jesus Christ. Likewise, they should keep a full affirmation of confidence in Jesus and firmly believe that He is ready to carry them to definite salvation and association with God in paradise. Timeless life is the gift that God All-powerful offers to us when we give our life to him. Timeless life is a heavenly kind of life, a daily existence that liberates us from the force of transgression and Satan. Eliminates on the basis of what is more, natural so we might know God and keep an individual relationship with Him until the end of time.

The basic quality of the mischievous is that they love obscurity because what they craft with their hands is insidious; they discover joy in wrongdoing and all types of impropriety. The trusting Christians who are brought back to life, they love nobility and disdain evil. They lament when they see the corrupt deeds of debased individuals. They deplore the corrupt leaders on the planet.

Chapter Thirteen

Jesus Christ's Earthly Ministry of Redemption & Teaching

Jesus Christ began His earthly ministry with the power of the Holy Spirit. He was rejected in Nazareth, where He was born and raised and grew up; according to the Scripture: "He went to Nazareth, where He had been brought up, and on the Sabbath day, he went into the synagogue, as was his custom. And he stood up to read. The scroll of the prophet Isaiah was handed to him, unrolling it; he found the place where it is written: The Spirit of the Lord is on me because he has anointed me to preach good news to the poor. He has sent me to proclaim freedom for the prisoners and recovery of sight for the blind. To release the oppressed, to proclaim the year of the Lord's favor" (Luke 4:16-19)

Jesus Christ was anointed by the Holy Spirit, He was empowered by the Holy Spirit. He came to the world as a result of the power of God's Spirit. He was conceived by the Holy Spirit and born from the womb of Virgin Mary. The miraculous conception of His birth is the clear proof that Jesus is a Holy God.

God, the Father Almighty, spoke Jesus into the womb of Virgin Mary, just as he spoke the earth into existence when the Spirit of God was hovering on the face of the waters. Similarly, the spirit of God was hovering on the face of the Earth, and God almighty spoke Jesus Christ into existence right into the womb of the Virgin Mary.

This is the reason why Jesus Christ had the incredible worth and strength to take the guilt of our sins on himself and was able to make atonement for them. Without a perfect, sinless Savior, we would not be redeemed of our sins and death. The Spirit of God came upon Jesus Christ in the form of a Dove to equip him with great power to perform his ministry. Along with that, he also had the noble work of redemption to do. The redemptive work of Jesus Christ reflects upon the purpose of His ministry, which was anointed by the Spirit. The purpose was to preach the gospel to the poor, the ones in destitute, the afflicted ones, the humble ones. To guide and support those crushed in the spirit, the brokenhearted, and those who tremble at His word. Jesus was here to heal those who were bruised and oppressed. Jesus Christ's healing power was accumulated in his real presence, as the whole person, both physically and spiritually. Jesus came into the world to open the spiritual eyes of those who are blinded by the world and Satan so that they might see the truth of God's good news. Jesus Christ's ministry was made to proclaim the time of true freedom and salvation from Satan's domain, sin, fear, and guilt. All the people on earth and Christian believers that are filled with the spirit, are called to share Jesus Christ's ministry in these ways. All believing Christians must gain a deep realization of the terrible temptations and misery that emerge from sin and the power of Satan. They must be aware of the condition of bondage to evil, broken heartedness, spiritual blindness, and physical distress.

Jesus Christ's first priority in His ministry was

to destroy the work of the devil. There can be no realization and acceptance of the kingdom of God without confronting the kingdom of Satan.

One unmistakable sign tells us that the kingdom has ceased to manifest among God's people, and that is the failure to directly confront the power of evil by setting sinners free from the bondage of sin and death. Jesus Christ was sent to the world to destroy the work of all evils and demonic power.

He was sent to the world to set the captives free. The Scripture says about Jesus Christ: "Then he rolled up the scroll, gave it back to the attendant and sat down. The eyes of everyone in the synagogue were fastened on him, and he began by saying to them, today, His scripture is fulfilled in your hearing."(Luke 4:20-21)

Jesus Christ has the freedom, capability, power, and right to decide or act. He often used the power in many jurisdictions of Satan's domain. The authority of Jesus Christ was the ultimate divine authority given by His Father in heaven. It came from the awareness of the Father's action, knowing what the Father was doing, and, therefore, involved the Father's endorsement. Jesus Christ delegated spiritual authority and power to all believers. However, Christ did not want believers to become authoritarian. He warned them not to be like rulers and officials of this world who exercise authority in a wicked terrorizing way, to dominate the people under them for worldly pleasures. During his earthly ministry, Jesus Christ used his authority and power to serve others, help people, heal the sick, instruct, and deliver demon-possessed people. Jesus Christ teaches the gospel of God boldly and clearly. He is the best teacher the world has ever known. There can be no one before Him, no one after Him. Jesus Christ preaches the good news of the kingdom of heaven; according to the Scripture: "But he said: I must preach the good news of the kingdom of God to the other towns also because that is why I was sent. And he kept on preaching in the synagogues of Judea."(Luke 4:43-44)

Jesus Christ made the reason for his arrival in this world clear to the people. The kingdom carries the idea of God, God the Father plans it, God the Son carries it out. God coming into the world to show and assert His power reflects His glory and rights against Satan's dominion and all his devilish angels from the present evil world. It was the gift of salvation to the church; God expressing himself powerfully in all His redemptive works. The kingdom of God is an assertion to ascertain the power of God in action on this earth. Through His incarnate begotten Son, God Almighty began His spiritual rule on earth, preaching the hearts and minds of His people. Jesus Christ, the Son of God, came to the world with power. The haters and enemies of God and the people of God will continue to be in the same world till the end of this age. Therefore, God ascertains Himself with power. The world will continue to enter into crises. The expression of the power of God's will fills Satan's empire with alarm. There will be a time everyone will be confronted with the decision of whether they submit to the rule of God or not. The necessary, fundamental conditions that will help the people of this world to enter into the kingdom of God are very simple and precise. These conditions only originate through the repentance of sins and believing in the gospel of God through Jesus Christ for salvation. The future manifestation of the glory of God, His power, and His kingdom will occur when Jesus Christ returns to judge the dead and the living in the world. The ultimate goal of fulfilling the kingdom will be achieved when Jesus Christ finally triumphs over evil and all its opposition's work and hands over the kingdom to God the Father, and God will be all in all: "Then the end will come when he hands over the kingdom to God the Father after he has destroyed all dominions, authority, and power. For he must reign until he has put all his enemy under his feet. The last enemy to be destroyed is death." (1st Corinthians 15:24-26)

It is essential for all believing Christians to diligently preserve the essence of God's love and surrender themselves completely to the Lordship of Jesus Christ. They have to actively seek the kingdom of God with their whole hearts and minds by living a life that honors His name and a life that is pleasing in His sight. All the believing Christians must pray for everything they need or everything they might be going through, without ceasing. Let us cast all our care upon Him, the one that promise is faithful. Jesus Christ, during his Earthly ministry, healed the sick, opened the eyes of the man born blind, He taught Nicodemus. The Scripture revealed: "Now there was a man of the Pharisees named Nicodemus, a member of the Jewish ruling council. He came to Jesus at night and said, Rabbi, we know you are a teacher who has come from God, for no one could perform the miraculous signs you are doing if God were not with him. In reply Jesus declared, I tell you the truth, no one can see the kingdom of God unless he is born again. How can a man be born when he is old? Nicodemus asked. Surely he cannot enter a second time into his mother's womb to be born! Jesus answered, I tell you the truth, and no one can enter the kingdom of God unless he is born of water and the spirit. Flesh gives birth to flesh, but the Spirit gives birth to spirit. You should not be surprised at my saying; you must be born again. The wind blows where it comes from or where it is going. So it is with everyone born of the spirit."(John 3:1-8)

The wind is the Spirit; as the wind, though unseen, is identified by its activity and sound. So also, the Holy Spirit is observed by His activity in and effect on those who are born again. Our Lord Jesus Christ teaches the gospel truthfully and clearly to Nicodemus the Pharisees. Our Lord Jesus Christ teaches Nicodemus the foundation of the Christian faith, which is about being born again and spiritual birth. Without being born again of Spirit, no one can enter the kingdom of God or receive eternal life and the gift of salvation, which is in Christ Jesus, Our Lord. Being born after the new birth, eternal life from God himself will be imparted to the believing Christians' hearts, and he or she will become a child of God—a new creation in Christ. Created to be like God in true righteousness and holiness, he or she will be able to follow the commandment of God and live a life that is pleasing and justified in His sight. Nicodemus' heart was changed to the point that he was there on the day of Christ's crucifixion and helped in preparing for

Christ's burial.

According to the Scripture, Jesus Christ preached to the Samaritan woman: "When a Samaritan woman came to draw water, Jesus said, to her, will you give a drink? (His disciples had gone into the town to buy food.) The Samaritan woman said to him, you are a Jew, and I am a Samaritan woman. How can you ask me for a drink? (For Jews do not associate with the Samaritans.) Jesus answered her, If you knew the gift of God and who it is that asks you for a drink, you would have asked him, and he would have given you living water. Sir, the woman said, you have nothing to draw with, and the well is deep. Are you greater than our Father Jacob, who gave us the well and drank from it himself, as did also his sons and his flocks and herds? Jesus answered, everyone who drinks this water will be thirsty again, but whoever drinks the water I give him will never thirst. Indeed, the water I give him will become in him a spring of water welling up to eternal life" (John 4: 7-14)

Our Lord Jesus Christ's conversation with the

Samaritan woman reveals His commitment to his heavenly Father's purpose. It also explains His inner desire to bring people to eternal life. Jesus Christ's consuming passion was to save the lost; it was an infinitely important goal to Him. He even prioritized it over food, drink, and all other necessities of daily life. All the believing Christians must follow Christ's example. All around us, people are ready to hear the word of God. We must find ways to speak to them about their spiritual need and about Jesus Christ, who can meet that need. The water Jesus Christ wants to give to those in need possesses a spiritual life. To benefit from this living water, progressive or repeated drinking is important, which requires regular communion with the source of the living water, Jesus Christ himself. No one can continue to drink the water of life if he or she becomes severed from its source; such people will become, as Apostle Peter describes it, "Springs without water."(2 Peter 2:17)

Jesus Christ taught and preached as the gospel during His earthly ministry. Christ also healed the sick. Jesus Christ healed the man that was born blind. The Holy Scripture reveals: "As he went along, he saw a man blind from birth. His disciples asked Rabbi, who sinned, this man or his parents, that he was born blind? Neither this man nor his parents sinned, said Jesus, but this happened so that the work of God might be displayed in his life. As long as it is day, we must do the work of him who sent me. Night is coming, when no one can work. While I am in the world, I am the light of the world. Having said this, he spit on the ground, made some mud with the saliva, and put it on the man's eyes. Go, he told him, wash in the pool of Siloam (this word means sent). So the man went and washed, and came home seeing." (John 9:1-7)

Jesus Christ taught, corrected, and explained to His disciples about their beliefs. He told them that not every serious affliction is always the result of sin. Some sicknesses do happen for other reasons and are not a result of our sin. Sometimes, God might permit long suffering because of a divine purpose or to display His mercy, love, and power to the people of this world. Most of the time, the innocent people of this world suffer, while the wicked people get away with their wickedness.

Jesus Christ healed blind Bartimaeus; he received his sight on the road to Jericho. The Scripture reveals: "Then they came to Jericho. As Jesus and his disciples, together with a large crowd, were leaving the city, a blind man, Bartimaeus (that is, the son of Timaeus), was sitting by the roadside begging. When he heard that it was Jesus of Nazareth, he began to shout, Jesus, Son of David, have mercy on me! Many rebuked him and told him to be quiet, but he shouted all the more, Son of David, have mercy on me! Jesus Stopped and said, Call him. So, they called to the blind man, Cheer up! On your feet! He's calling you. Throwing his cloak aside, he jumped to his feet and came to Jesus. What do you want me to do for you? Jesus asked him. The blind man said, Rabbi, I want to see. Go, said Jesus, your faith has healed you. Immediately he received his sight and followed Jesus along the road." (Mark 10:46-52)

Our Lord Jesus Christ showed His compassion to the blind Bartimaeus. On the road to Jericho, He heard his voice and stopped. Jesus told them to bring the man to Him. Ours was a compassionate God, full of truth and righteousness, and He is the same even today. If you call Him faithfully and sincerely, he will answer your prayers, fulfill your need and solve your problems.

Jesus Christ paid the ransom for our sins. The ransom conveys the price that Christ paid in order to obtain freedom for us; through His redemptive work, his death is the price paid for the release of people in this world from the dominion of sin and death. Jesus Christ, during His earthly ministerial work, wakes up the death. According to the Holy Scripture: "While He was saying this, a ruler came and knelt before him and said, my daughter has just died. But come and put your hand on her, and she will live. Jesus got up and went with him, and so did His disciples. Just then, a woman who had been subject to bleeding for twelve years came up behind him and touched the edge of his cloak. She said to herself, if I only touch his cloak, I will be healed. Jesus turned and saw her. Take heart daughter, he said, your faith has healed you. And the woman was healed from that moment. When Jesus entered the ruler's house and saw the flute players and noisy crowd, he said, go away. The girl is not dead but asleep. But they laughed at him. After the crowd had been put outside, he went in and took the girl by the hand, and she got up. News of this spread through all the region." (Matthew 9:18-25)

We can see how powerful our Lord is on Earth. Even the Scripture says that when evening came, many demon-possessed were brought to him, and he drove out the spirits with a word and healed all the sick.

This was to fulfill what was spoken through the prophet Isaiah: "He took up our infirmities and carried our diseases."(Matthew 8:16-17)

Jesus Christ solved the problems of sickness and diseases because He knows that our sin causes all our diseases and illnesses. Sins affect humanity spiritually and physically. Satan also uses sins to torture the people in the world.

The provision of God in redemption is as extensive as the consequence of the fall in the Garden of Eden. God provides forgiveness for sin and death, and He is also the one to provide resurrection and the gift of eternal life. God blesses us with divine healing for sickness and diseases through Jesus Christ, our Lord, and Savior. Christ came and manifested the ministry of teaching, preaching, and healing for then and forever; it continues even today. Jesus Christ healed the woman who had been bleeding for good twelve years with His word. Jesus touches the sick, and the sick touch Jesus. The contact and the presence of Jesus Christ matter in our lives. Christ's touch has healing power because he sympathizes with our infirmities and our weaknesses; He is the source of life and grace. Our main goal and responsibility are to seek to be near Him as we look for healing. We must learn to live in His presence with faith and belief in His power.

On that same day, Jesus wakes up Jairu's daughter with one word—the daughter of the synagogue ruler who died. Jesus told her father when people were mocking him about the child being already dead. Jesus responded that his daughter was asleep. He encouraged the child's father in a seemingly hopeless situation.

Throughout the redemptive history, Christian believers were instructed and expected to place their faith and trust in God the Father, Son, and the Holy Spirit one God forever, even when it seemed as if all was lost and there was no hope. In such a time, God gave the necessary faith and delivered His people according to His will and His purpose.

Jesus Christ healed the woman and raised the ruler's daughter with two words "Talitha koum!" which means "Little girl get up." She walked around, and Jesus told them to give her something to eat to show how healthy the child was after Jesus raised her from the dead.

Jesus Christ also woke up Lazarus. The Scripture says: "His sisters sent a word to Jesus saying that, Lord, the one you love is sick. When he heard this, Jesus said, This sickness will not end in death. No, it is for God's glory so that God's Son may be glorified through it. So, then he told them plainly, Lazarus is dead, and for your sake, I am glad I was not there, so that you may believe. But let us go to him Lord, Martha said to Jesus, if you had been here, my brother would not have died, but I know that even now God will give you whatever you ask. Jesus said to her, your brother will rise again. Martha answered, I know he will rise again in the resurrection at the last day. Jesus said to her, I am the resurrection and the life. He who believes in me will live, even though he dies, and whoever lives and believes in me will never die. Do you believe this? Yes, Lord, she told him, I believe that you are the Christ, the son of God, who was to come into the world. (John 11: 1-2a, 3-4, 14, 21-27)

Our Lord Jesus Christ said that Lazarus' sickness is for the glory of God. Sickness among the people of God will never result in death as the outcome. Death ultimately will be destroyed by resurrection.

The Scripture says: "When Jesus saw her weeping, and the Jews who had come along with her, also weeping, he was deeply moved in spirit and troubled. Where have you laid him? He asked. Come and see, Lord, they replied. Jesus wept. Then the Jews said, see how he loved him" (John 11: 33-36)

The Scripture further reveals: "Jesus, once more deeply moved, came to the tomb. It was a cave with a stone laid across the entrance. Take away the stone, he said. But, Lord, said Martha, the sister of the dead man, by this time there is a bad odor, for he has been there four days. Then Jesus said, did I not tell you that if you believed, you would see the glory of God. So, they took away the stone. Then Jesus looked up and said, Father, I thank you that you have heard me, I knew that you always hear me, but I said this for the benefit of the people standing here, that they may believe that you sent me. When he had said this, Jesus called in a loud voice, Lazarus, come out! The dead man came out, his hands and feet wrapped with strips of linen, and a cloth around his face. Jesus said to them, take off the grave clothes and let him Go."(John 11: 38-44)

Jesus Christ loved Mary and Martha. When we suffer or are sick, it does not mean that Jesus does not love us. Jesus loved Mary, Martha, and their brother, Lazarus, and all of them loved Jesus. They all shared a strong relationship, affection, and devotion with Christ, but they experienced sorrow, sickness, and death.

Even in the current times, these troubles can and will happen to God's faithful and chosen Christian believers, the people of God. Delay from Jesus Christ is not a lack of love, mercy, or compassion; it is for the glory of God and His kingdom and the ultimate eternal good of the sufferers. Our confidence must not rest or depend on what God is letting happen in the current time. Instead, we must keep our focus on the immensity of His identity and His power and love in our lives. There are Seven Miracles that the Lord Jesus Christ performed during his earthly ministry, and these miracles made it clear who Jesus Christ is,

the Son of God to the world.

155

Chapter Fourteen

Jesus Christ Crucifixion And Resurrection

The most significant thing that happened in this world was the crucifixion, death, burial, and the resurrection of our Lord Jesus Christ. The Holy scripture revealed: "Yet it was the Lord's will to crush him and cause him to suffer, and though the Lord makes his life a guilt offering, he will see his offspring and prolong his days, and the will of the Lord will prosper in his hand. After the suffering of his soul, he will see the light of life and be satisfied. By his knowledge, my righteous servant will justify many, and he will bear their iniquities. Therefore, I will give him a portion among the great, and he will divide the spoils with the strong because he poured out his life unto death and was numbered with transgressors. For he bore the sin of many and made intercession for the transgressors."(Isaiah 53:10-12)

God the Father's will for His Son was to come to

the world and bought us with His precious blood for our sins. It is the will of God the Father that His Son is sent to the world to die on the cross for the lost universe. By making Jesus Christ an atoning sacrifice for all our transgressions and Sin, God showed us He is the one who Has control over all the decisions in the world. The will of God is also used to designate anything as per His desires. God wants everyone in this universe to be saved and and not to fall from grace. The will of God may also be referred to as what God permits or allows to happen. It may also be called God's permissive order or God's permissive will. By making Christ atone for our sins, God showed us mercy. The purpose of the atonement was to provide a comprehensive sacrifice for all the sins of humanity. Therefore, the people of this world will be cleansed from their sins of the past, present, and future. It brings us to hope that we may maintain fellowship with God. The Day of Atonement symbolizes and points towards the Mediatorial Ministry and atoning the death of Christ Jesus. Christ's death on the cross fulfilled the prophecy and bought human beings freedom from bondage and slavery to sin. By his burial, Jesus Christ removed the doubt that he had died.

It showed us that if we trust and have faith in Him, He will raise us from the dead and bless us with an immortal body. The resurrection of Jesus Christ is the greatest proof that He is indeed the true incarnate Son of God. Jesus Christ's death, burial, and resurrection are the very foundation of the gospel of God.

"Pilate called together the chief priests, the rulers, and the people, and said to them, you brought me this man as one who was inciting the people to rebellion. I have examined him in your presence and have found no basis for your charges against him. Neither has Herod, for he sent him back to us; as you can see, he has done nothing to deserve death. Therefore, I will punish him and then release him. With one voice they cried out, away with this man! Release Barabbas to us! (Barabbas had been thrown into prison for an insurrection in the city and murder) Wanting to release Jesus, Pilate appealed to them again. But they kept shouting. Crucify him!

Crucify!"(Luke 23:13-20)

Jesus was accused of treason against Rome. Pilate concludes that Jesus Christ was innocent of any rebellion against the Roman government. Jesus Christ declared that His kingdom is not a political kingdom of this world, but a spiritual one. Jesus Christ was crucified. The crucifixion and the death of Jesus are the core foundation of the plan of God for redemption. Jesus, who had never sinned, died on behalf of the sinful human race. Through Christ's crucifixion, the penalty for our sin got paid completely. God put an end to the work of Satan from the Garden of Eden.

From then onwards and even now, people of this world may turn to God in repentance and faith and receive the forgiveness of their sins. They may be granted the peace of eternal life only because of Christ Jesus our Redeemer King. The Scripture revealed: "Now there was a man named Joseph, a member of the Council, a good and upright man, who had not consented to their decision and action.

He came from the Judean town of Arimathea, and he was waiting for the Kingdom of God. Going to Pilate he asked for Jesus ' body. Then he took it down, wrapped it in a linen cloth, and placed it in a tomb cut in the rock, one in which no one had yet been laid. It was Preparation Day, and the Sabbath was about to begin."(Luke 23: 50-54)

A wealthy man, Joseph from the village of Arimathea, asked permission from Pilate to bury the body of Jesus in his new tomb where nobody ever laid before. Jesus Christ was buried on Friday before the Sabbath began. The tomb had been hewn out of solid rock. It was probably large enough to walk into but with a low entrance. After placing the body of Christ in the tomb, Joseph Arimathea rolled a big stone in front of its entrance.

The Scripture speaks of the resurrection of Jesus Christ: "On the first day of the week, very early in the morning, the women took the spices they had prepared and went to the tomb. They found the stone rolled away from the tomb, but when they entered, they did not find the body of the Lord Jesus. While they were wondering about this, suddenly two men in clothes that gleamed like lightning stood beside them. In their fright, the women bowed down with their faces on the ground, but the men said to them, why do you look for the living among the dead? He is not here; he has risen! Remember how he told you while he was still with you in Galilee. The Son of man must be delivered into the hands of sinful men, be crucified, and on the third day be raised again. Then they remembered his words. When they came back from the tomb, they told all these things to the eleven and to all the others. It was Mary Magdalene, Joanna, Mary the mother of James and the other with them who told this to the apostle."(Luke 24:1-10)

Jesus Christ is an active agent before the foundation of the world. Jesus Christ is always with the Father, just as He is seated at the right hand of the throne of God the Father even right now and reigning in the unity of the Holy Spirit one God forever and ever. God the Father says it, Jesus Christ carries it, and the Holy Spirit will empower it. The Holy Scripture reveals: "He is the image of the invisible God, the firstborn over all creation. For by him, all things were created: things in heaven and on earth, visible and invisible, whether thrones or powers or rulers or authorities; all things were created by him and for him. He is before all things, and in him, all things hold together." (Colossians 1:15-17)

Jesus Christ is the firstborn of all creation. It means that Christ Jesus is the supreme heir; He is the heir and the ruler of all creations because he is the eternal Son. Through Jesus Christ, all things in heaven and on earth were created.

Apostle Paul gave a clear affirmation of the creative activities of Jesus Christ before the foundation of the world. All things were created for Him. Through Him, all the material, physical, and spiritual world came into existence. All the objects, creatures, and realms owe their existence to Jesus Christ's creative work as He was an active agent in creation. All these are held together and sustained in Christ Jesus. God Almighty created all things through Jesus Christ. Jesus Christ is the eternal word of God. Through Him, all things were made; without Him, nothing would have been made. By Christ Jesus, all things were created; all things were made—visible and invisible. All things were created by Him and for Him.

The book of the Hebrews revealed: "In the past, God spoke to our forefathers through the prophets at many times and in various ways, but in these last days he has spoken to us by his Son, unto us by his Son whom he appointed heir of all things, and through whom he made the universe. The Son is the radiance of God's glory and the exact representation of his being, sustaining all things by His powerful Word. After he had provided purification for sin, he sat down at the right hand of the Majesty in the heavens." (Hebrews 1:1-3)

The gospel of John gave an account of how Mary Magdalene went back alone: "Then the disciples went back to their homes. But Mary stood outside the tomb crying. As she wept, she bent over to look into the tomb and saw two angels in white, seated where Jesus' body had been, one at the head and the other at the foot. They asked her, woman, why are you crying? They have taken my Lord away, she said, and I don't know where they put him. At this, she turned around and saw Jesus standing there, but she did not realize that it was Jesus. Woman, he said, why are you crying? Who is it you are looking for? Thinking he was the Gardner, she said, Sir, if you have carried him away, tell me where you have put him, and I will get him. Jesus said to her, Mary, she turned toward him and cried out in Aramaic Rabboni. Jesus said, do not hold on to me, for I have not yet returned to the Father. Go instead to my brothers and tell them, I am returning to my Father and your Father, to my God and your God. Mary Magdalene went to the disciples with the news: I have seen the Lord! And she told them that he had said these things to her." (John 20:10-18)

Through the power of the Holy Spirit, Jesus Christ was raised from the grave and thereby vindicated as the true Messiah and the true Son of God. Through the power of the Holy Spirit, Jesus Christ was declared to be the son of God. The Spirit raised Jesus from the grave and thereby vindicated him as the true Messiah and the true Son of God. Through the power of the Holy Spirit, Jesus Christ was declared to be the Son of God. The Spirit raised Jesus from the dead as Jesus responded to His power only. Christ depended on the Holy Spirit for his resurrection. Therefore, all believing in Christ must rely on the Holy Spirit's power to attain spiritual life on this earth. They must look forward to the bodily resurrection in the life to come.

In the future, Jesus Christ's resurrection is confirmed by the following facts.

(1) The tomb was empty by the time the women went there: If the enemies of Jesus had taken him or possessed his body, they indeed would have displayed it to prove that he had not risen.

If the disciples had taken his body, they would have never sacrificed their lives and possession for what they knew to be false. The empty tomb reveals that Jesus did arise and was truly the Son of God.

(2) The existence, power, joy, and devotion of the early church: If Jesus had not risen and appeared to them, they would have never been able to reach unheard-of joy, courage, and hope from the darkness of deep despair and loss of hope.

(3) The writing by men giving their lives for the truth and righteousness taught by Jesus: They would never have taken the trouble to write about a Messiah and His teaching if His ministry had ended in death and disillusionment.

(4) The baptism in the Holy Spirit and His manifestation within the church: The Holy Spirit was poured out at Pentecost as an experiential reality. It is proof that Jesus had risen and was exalted at the right hand of God. If Jesus Christ had not risen, there would have been no experiential of baptism in the Holy Spirit.

(5) There have been millions of people throughout

the last 2,000-years who experienced in their hearts and lived the presence of Jesus Christ: There are people who have witnessed the presence of Holy Spirit as well. The first person to whom Jesus Christ appears after his resurrection was Mary Magdalene. She is not a particularly prominent person in the gospel, yet Jesus Christ appears first to her rather than to any of the outstanding leaders among the disciples. Up till his day, and throughout the ages, Jesus Christ reveals His presence and love, especially to the lowly. God's special people are unknown. They are the people like Mary those who, in their grief, maintain a steadfast love for their Lord. Christ told Mary, Do not hold on to me yet; I am not yet ascended to my Father; you will still have the opportunity to see me again. He gave her a message to go and tell the good news to the apostle. Our Lord gave us the great commission to take the good news of the gospel to the people on Earth. Jesus Christ has risen; He has risen indeed.

He is alive forever. Jesus Christ resurrection from the dead is for all believers' justification; the

Holy Scripture revealed: "He was delivered over to death for our sins and was raised to life for our justification."(Roman 4:25)

We were therefore buried with him through baptism into death so that, just as Christ was raised from the dead through the glory of the Father, we too may live a new life.

"And if the Spirit of him who raised Jesus from the dead is living in you, he who raised Christ from the dead will also give life to your mortal bodies through his Spirit, who lives in you."(Romans 8:11)

"That if you confess with your mouth, Jesus is Lord, and believe in your heart that God raised him from the dead, you will be saved. For it is with your heart that you believed and are justified, and it is with your mouth that you confess and are saved."(Roman 10: 9-10)

God Almighty Father exhibited His power by raising our Lord Jesus Christ, the only begotten Son, from the grave. God has the power, but He can be counted on to use His power to accomplish His purposes and desire. He uses His power to keep his promises and fulfill his promises in our lives. Justification and righteousness come through God's mercy, grace, love, and forgiveness.

Abraham's faith, his belief, his attachment to God, his strong confidence, and unwavering assurance in God and his promises was credited as righteousness by the mercy and grace of God.

All believing Christians were buried with Jesus Christ through baptism. The water of baptism for believers represents the guarantee of their burial and resurrection with Jesus Christ, but it is even more. When accompanied by true faith, baptism becomes our medium of resurrection with Jesus Christ. Baptism is part of our rejection of sin and our commitment to Christ, resulting in a continual flow after death and divine life to us. Baptism means identifying with Jesus Christ in His death, burial, and resurrection so that we may live in union with His resurrected life. As Christ rose from the dead, so are we blessed with the surety that those who exercise saving faith in Him will walk in the newness of life. We, believers of Jesus Christ, were once controlled by sinful nature, but the moment the Spirit of God resided in us, we received a spiritual birth. We were blessed with the faith that Jesus Christ have the Holy Spirit living in us. The indwelling presence of the Spirit is related to the new birth; the baptism in the Holy Spirit is an empowering experience related to initiation that leads to exploring charismatic gifts. The body in its natural state is under the process of death, even for the Christian believers, because of the sins and their ravaging effects. Our bodies ultimately will be redeemed by the resurrection from the transformation at Jesus Christ's second coming to the earth.

Because Christ Jesus came to the world to give us life here and now, the Holy Spirit who raised Jesus from the dead desires to impart life to our mortal bodies. as we embrace His life within us – The holy Spirit's the spirit of life.

God raised Christ from the dead; anyone that does not believe in Christ's bodily resurrection cannot claim to be a Christian or believer of Jesus Christ. He or she would be an unbeliever because the death and the resurrection of Jesus Christ is the central event in Salvation. Jesus Christ is specifically called Savior and Lord; no one can receive Jesus as Savior without receiving him as Lord. This is fundamental education and is as significant as the proclamation of the gospel. As a Ruler, Jesus Christ has power, territory, authority, and the option to dominate everything. Jesus is Master; He is pronounced equivalent to God. He is the one who is deserving of all the force, love, trust, compliance, and supplication. When we call Jesus "Ruler", it is an outward acceptance as well as a true internal disposition of the heart that they made Jesus and his statement Lord over all of creation and life. Jesus should be Master at home and in the congregations and every one of our connections, just as He should be in scholarly, monetary, training, sporting, professional, and every other part of our lives. Christ Jesus should be the Ruler of all.

Chapter Fifteen

Christ's Promise of the Holy Spirit Fulfilled

Holy Spirit at Pentecost: The Holy Spirit descended on the apostles on the day of the Passover Sabbath, called the feast of harvest. Hence, it is one of the great Jewish festivals that people celebrate with other nations in Jerusalem. The Holy Spirit descended like rushing wind; which exactly, resembled the breath of God that evoked life in human beings before that; humans did not exist. Similarly, the church did not have a live existence until God breathed the Holy Spirit on the apostles, with the sign of wind and fire like a tongue. The tongue of fire symbolizes the presence of God. It is basically the representation of the Holy Spirit.

The flames of fire symbolize the purity and the power they needed to preach, teach, and proclaim the gospel of God clearly and boldly. They needed all this to clearly let the people know what Jesus Christ has done before He went back to the presence of God; seated at God's right hand.

God Almighty Father gave the disciples supernatural powers. He gifted them the Spirit to speak and understand languages they had never heard, studied, or known before. It was the ability of those people to speak in any languages that gathered all the people from all the nations under heaven for the Jewish feast of harvest in Jerusalem.

The Holy Spirit's presence signified baptism into the spiritual body, which is church, the body of Christ. The gift of tongue fluency in other languages was given to the apostles. It is also given to some of us today in order to enable us to do the missionary work. It is for us to accomplish a particular purpose for the Lord; we have to devote ourselves to preaching and teaching the gospel to all the people in all the nations.

The same God has done everything in the lives of Israelites. He has shown them His glory by parting the Red Sea and making them walk out in a dry land. He made the wall of Jericho fell down and fed them in the wilderness with Manner and Quale from heaven. He brought the water out of the rock in the wilderness. The same God fulfilled His promise by descending the Holy Spirit from heaven like a rushing wind and empowered the apostles to preach the gospel, and more than three thousand souls were saved. God the Holy Trinity one God forever is the God of love; He is still saving souls of the sinners and the lost through the power of the Holy Spirit until today and will continues until He returns to judge the dead and the living.

Today's Ministers of the gospel were able to speak and understand the languages of people of other nations because it is the Holy Spirit who gave the utterance of understanding of the languages of all the nations of the universe. On the day of Pentecost, the people in Jerusalem worshiped the Lord God for His power, which was displayed among them on that day. We have to pray that the Holy Trinity will continue to send His Holy Spirit to us with the power of tongue of fire, so that we can take the gospel to all the people in all the nations of this world in their own languages. It will enable us to bring the gospel's proclamation to the end of the earth and in their respective languages before Christ returns.

The promise of the Holy Spirit from Old Testament to the New Testament which God the Father laid upon Jesus Christ before His ascension into heaven. The Father put everything, including the things in heaven and on earth, under His feet. He appointed Christ as the head over everything and the church. We must remember that the Church is the body that fills all things in every way in heaven and on earth.

Jesus Christ, our Lord and Savior, ascended into heaven. He is our mediator of the new covenant. He is praying for us. He understood our problems because He was human like us and lived on this earth with us. He was the one who take all our infirmities. Ascension is always on Thursdays. All the believing Christians celebrate the ascension of Jesus into heaven according to the Holy Scripture that says Jesus' promise of the Holy Spirit was revealed to the disciple in words: "I am going to send you what my Father has promised; but stay in the city until you have been clothed with power from on high." (Luke 24:49)

The Lord Jesus Christ reminded the apostles about the promise of the Father: what my Father has promised that will he will do. He will pour power from above refers to the outpouring of the Holy Spirit that began at Pentecost. The same promise of the Father was revealed in the Old Testament in the book of Isaiah the Prophet: "Till the Spirit is poured upon us from on high, and the desert becomes a fertile field, and the fertile field seems like a forest." (Isaiah 32:15) Prophet Isaiah was given the same vision of the coming of the Holy Spirit and the righteous reign of the King. The age of righteousness and the blessing of the kingdom will arrive when the Holy Spirit is poured out upon the people of God from heaven.

In another Scripture, the Lord said: "For I will pour water on the thirsty Land, and streams on the dry ground; I will pour out my Spirit on your offspring and my blessings on your descendants" (Isaiah 44:3)

We read here again that the Lord mentioned His

promise of outpouring His Spirit upon His people as well as their descendants. Prophet Isaiah prophesied that the day would come when the Holy Spirit will be poured out on the future generations of Israelites and upon all the people on earth that called on His Holy name faithfully and sincerely. This prophecy of Prophet Isaiah was fulfilled on the day of Pentecost. The complete fulfillment for the people of Israel will occur after they accept Jesus Christ as their Messiah. The outpouring of God's Spirit upon His people is associated with restoration, blessing, and fruitfulness. The result of the outpouring of the Holy Spirit depends on the testimony that we belong to the Lord Jesus Christ, and He is our heavenly Father. The Holy Spirit created the confidence and assurance in us that we are one in Him. We belongs to God the Holy Trinity forever one God; we have all the benefits and privileges as a joint heir of Christ as the children. In the book of prophet Ezekiel, the Scripture says: "I will no longer hide my face from them, for I will pour out my Spirit on the house of Israel, declared the sovereign Lord" (Ezekiel 39:29)

In the book of Joel, the Lord's promise was revealed once again: "And afterward, I will pour out my Spirit on all people. Your sons and daughters will prophesy; your old men will dream dreams, your young men will see visions. Even on my servants, both men and women, I will pour out my Spirit those days" (Joel 2:28-29)

Apostle Peter quoted this passage on the Day of Pentecost, explaining to the people from all the nations that filled the city of Jerusalem on that day. Out pouring of the Holy Spirit on that day was the beginning of the fulfillment of Joel's prophecy. Even apostle Peter mentioned the prediction of Prophet Joel on the day of Pentecost. Joel predicts a day when God will pour out his Spirit on everyone who calls on his name. This outpouring will result in a charismatic flow of the Spirit and prophetic manifestations among the people of God. This prophecy is an ongoing event based on the promise of God to all who accept Jesus Christ as their Lord and Savior; all believers can be filled and should be filled with the Holy Spirit if they gave their lives to Christ in true holiness. Joel stated and envisioned that one of the primary results of the outpouring of the Holy Spirit will be the impartation and release of prophetic gifts. The manifestation of the Holy Spirit through his gifts makes known the presence of God among His people.

The full realization of this outpouring of the Spirit and the offer of salvation to all the people will happen by the end of time on the day of the Lord. At that time, the enemies of God will experience the wrath of God.

The outpouring of the Spirit of God was mentioned many times in the New Testament. The Scripture reveals that our Lord said: "And I will ask the Father, and he will give you another counselor to be with you forever - The Spirit of truth. The world cannot accept him because it neither sees him nor knows him. But you know him, for he lives with you and will be in you. I will not leave you as orphans; I will come to you but the counselor, the Holy Spirit, whom the Father will send in my name, will teach you all things and will remind you of everything I have said to you" (John 14:16-18, 26)

Our Lord Jesus Christ, before His ascension, reminded the apostle of the Father's promise, which He had made beforehand, during his earthly teaching ministry. Jesus Christ said that He will ask the Father to give the counselor only to those who are faithful and serious about their love for Him. It will be given to those who are truly devoted to His word. Our Lord continued to emphasize love, faithfulness, and obedience to his Word. The Spirit will be by the disciples' side. Today, it is with us to help us, straighten us, and teach the true course for our lives. It comforts the mind under challenging times and in all the problematic situations of lives.

The Holy Spirit will intercede for us in our prayers and pray for us; the Spirit will be a friend to further our best interest and remain with us forever. The Holy Spirit is called the spirit of truth because He is the spirit of Jesus. Jesus is the way of truth and the life. He testifies to the truth and enlightens us regarding the truth of everything, for He is the one who can expose all lies of the people in the world. He guides the Christian believers into all truth. Those who are willing to sacrifice truth for the sake of unity, love, or any other reason deny the Spirit of truth, who they claim lives in them. The church that abandons the truth of the word of God, abandons His Lord.

The Holy Spirit will not be the counselor of those who did not know the Lord. He will not support those who are indifferent to the faith and act half-heartedly in their commitment to the truth. The Holy Spirit comes only to those who worship the Lord in Spirit and in truth. Our Lord said that the Holy Spirit would live with disciples and those who belongs to Him. Jesus Christ promises the followers that He will be with us in the future. This is the promise that refers to the indwelling of the Holy Spirit that was fulfilled after Jesus Christ's resurrection. It was fulfilled when he breathed on them and asked them to receive the Holy Spirit.

"Again Jesus said, Peace be with you! As the Father has sent me, I am sending you. And with that, he breathed on them and said, receive the Holy Spirit. If you forgive anyone's sins, they are forgiven; if you do not forgive them, they are not forgiven" (John 20:21-

23).

In another Scripture: "But when he, the spirit of truth, comes, he will guide you into all truth. He will not speak of his own; he will speak only what he hears, and he will tell you what is yet to come. He will bring glory to me by taking from what is mine and making it known to you. All that belongs to the Father is mine. That is why I said the Spirit will take from what is mine and make it known to you" (John 16:13-15)

Those who are willing to receive the Holy Spirit must make themselves fully devoted to the Lord in Spirit and in truth. Jesus Christ will come to the believing Christians who are obedient to His word. He will be with those who faithfully follow Him through the power of the Holy Spirit, acknowledge the very presence of Christ, and believe He will be with the ones who love Him. The Holy Spirit will make them recognize the presence and the close proximity of Jesus Christ and the reality of His love, blessings, and supportive help. One of the Holy Spirit's primary tasks is to believe in Christ. The fact that Christ Jesus comes to us through the Holy Spirit should make us respond in love, worship, and devotion.

The Holy Spirit manifested his Holy character in the lives of all believing Christians, which is something that matters the most for believers. The counselor is the Holy Spirit. He is Holy; this is the most important reminder in the lives of all Christians because He always purifies us. He is the one that molds us to live a Christian life. He enables us to be consistent in maintaining a Christ-like character in our lives. The Scripture revealed: "But I tell you the truth: It is for your good that I am going away. Unless I go away, the counselor will not come to you; but if I go, I will send him to you. When he comes, he will convict the world of guilt in regard to sin and righteousness and judgment; in regard to sin, because men do not believe in me; in regard to righteousness, because I am going to the Father; where you can see me no longer; and in regard to judgment, because the prince of this world now stands condemned" (John 16:7-11)

Jesus Christ, again in this passage, promised

the fulfillment of the promise to send the Holy Spirit. He promised the outpouring of the Holy Spirit, which only happened after the departure of Jesus Christ back to heaven. When the Holy Spirit comes, his principal work would be to convict the world of sin, proclaiming the gospel of God through believing Christians. The Holy Spirit's ministry's purpose is to expose sin and hypocrisy to awaken the consciousness of sin and the need for forgiveness. The conviction will also clarify the fearful results if the guilty continue in their wrongdoing. This conviction will lead to true repentance, turning to Jesus Christ as Lord and Savior, and our righteousness. The Holy Spirit will convince people that Jesus Christ is the righteous Son of God, resurrected, vindicated, and now the Lord of all. He will make them aware of God's standard of righteousness in Jesus Christ, show them what sin is, and give them the power to overcome the world of sin. The Spirit will convict them of judgment. He will convince people of Satan's defeat at the cross, God's present judgment of the world, and the future judgment of all the people in the world.

The Spirit's work of convicting the people of sin, righteousness, and judgment will manifest in all who are baptized in the Holy Spirit and are truly Spirit-filled believers. Jesus Christ was filled with the Holy Spirit. He testified to the world that the world is filled with evil and called people to repent. John The Baptist was filled with Holy Spirit right from the womb. He exposed the sins of the Israelites, the people of Israel, and commanded them to change their ways. Apostle Peter was filled with the Holy Spirit and preached the gospel. Three thousand people were converted; he called them to repent of their sins and receive the forgiveness of sin. The Holy Spirit will guide people of this world who believe in Jesus Christ, and they will be saved. Holy Spirit works in the lives of believers and the church to teach, correct, and guide them into all truth. The Holy Spirit speaks to all the believieving Christians concerning sin, the righteousness of Jesus Christ, and the judgment of this evil world in order to conform them to Jesus Christ and his righteousness. It guides them into all truth and glorifies Jesus Christ. Therefore, the Holy Spirit works with believers. It resides inside the believers in order to remind them to be repentant and look at Jesus Christ's holy life in their lives as a reference. Only those who receive the truth and are led by the Spirit of God are sons and daughters of God, and they will therefore, be able to continue in the Spirit's fullness.

The Lord let the disciples know that the Father will fulfill His promise of the Holy Spirit, which they heard from Him. Christ said when He gets to heaven, He will ask the Father about His promise for His people. Jesus Christ is our advocate; He is the man between God and man. He is our great intercessor in heaven.

The Scripture revealed that the apostle staying in Jerusalem: "Do not leave Jerusalem, but wait for the gift my Father promised which you have heard me speak about. For John Baptized with water, but in a few days you will be baptized with the Holy Spirit." (Acts 1:4b-5)

It will be the gift of the Father's promise baptism of the Holy Spirit.

As per the promise, the disciple will be filled with the power of the Holy Spirit. Jesus Christ himself is the one who baptizes His believing Christians in the Holy Spirit. Our Lord said they would receive the power of the Holy Spirit; because the purpose of baptism in the Holy Spirit is receiving of power to witness for Jesus Christ. They are given the power so that the sinners and the lost sheep of this world are won over to Him and saved. They will be taught to obey all that Christ Jesus commanded in order for Him to be known, loved, praised, and be made the Lord of all the people of God on earth.

The chosen people of God will have more strength, ability, courage, and power to operate all the ministry work. The Holy Spirit's power includes driving demons and evil spirits away and healing the sick with the name of Jesus Christ through the power of the Holy Spirit. Holy Spirit's power will witness to the sinners and the lost without even saying a word because of the light of the power of the Holy Spirit that dwells in the believer. The Holy Spirit will make a loud and big proclamation of the gospel through the believers in a miraculous way that no one could ever imagine. Believers will witness boldly and clearly proclaim the love of God with great boldness; with great power, they will testify with many signs, wonders, and miracles.

The release of the Holy Spirit's power helps the believers to have the authority to drive out any evil spirits. The anointing to heal the sick are the two essential signs that accompany the proclamation of God's kingdom. The Baptism of the Holy Spirit increases the effectiveness of preaching. It provides enlightenment to introduce Jesus Christ as Lord and Savior. We also need it to increase the effectiveness of witness and strengthen and deepen the relationship with the Father, Son, and Holy Spirit. It all comes from being filled with the Spirit.

The Holy Spirit discloses and makes the personal presence of Jesus more real to us. It enables us to witness an intimate fellowship with Jesus Christ himself, resulting in an ever-growing desire on our part to love, honor and please our Savior and redeemer. The Holy Spirit witnesses righteousness and the truth that brings great glory to Jesus Christ, not only with words but also in deeds. Therefore, those who have received the witness of the Spirit that reveals Christ's redemptive work will manifest Christ-likeness, love, truth, and righteousness in their lives. The Baptism of the Holy Spirit is the initiation point whereby Spirit-filled believers receive the enabling power of the Holy Spirit to witness for Jesus Christ. The Baptism in the Holy Spirit can be given only to those believing Christians whose hearts are turned completely toward God in repentance of their sins.

The baptism in the Holy Spirit is the baptism to live a holy life. The Spirit of Holiness will dwell in the believer's hearts and minds, which will make the Spirit of truth work in all the fullness of God. The Spirit will be able to work in fact with greater conformity to Jesus Christ's holiness.

Baptism in the Holy Spirit will empower our prayers that cannot be uttered. The Holy Spirit will take our prayer request to the throne of grace, and believers will get their prayers answered through the power of the Holy Spirit.

The indwelling of the Holy Spirit assures us that

anything we ask in prayer will be done if the Lord knows that what we ask for in prayer is good for us and especially is according to His will, word, and commandment. The Scripture says: "They all joined together constantly in prayer, along with the women and Mary the mother of Jesus, and with his brothers" (Acts 1:14)

The apostles were with the women and the mother of Jesus, his brothers, and his sisters. They were all waiting and praying in the upper room for the fulfillment of the promise of the Father. It is a big responsibility for Christ's followers today. Those who are in need of the outpouring of the power to do the work of God should make themselves available to the Holy Spirit power manifestation. They should continue praying to the Lord until He baptizes them with the Holy Spirit. They should commit themselves to the will of God through unceasing prayer.

The Spirit power descends on believers according to the will of God. The example of the disciples can be seen by the way the Spirit descended upon them while they stayed in the upper room for ten days with constant prayers in Jerusalem. Christian believers of today must do the same to imitate the disciples. We must make ourselves available for prayer and supplication to the Lord until the Holy Spirit descends on us with power from heaven. We should call on the Lord Jesus

Christ to baptize us in the Holy Spirit. The ministry of Jesus Christ and the disciples started to work after the Spirit came upon them with power.

It is the same with us today. We must pray without ceasing until the Lord Jesus Christ connects us permanently with His Spirit. In order for us to serve Him boldly, clearly, faithfully, and sincerely according to His will, the Holy Spirit orders us to follow His commandment and faithfully do His Will for us. We have no power of our own without the baptism of the Holy Spirit; without it, we cannot fully serve the Lord.

We need the Spirit power in everything that we do or intend to do in the future. We need the power of Spirit especially to do the work required in the gospel ministry, as it cannot be done alone. We have to pray more and more, again and again, in order to be connected with the Spirit of Jesus Christ, which the Father promises.

As Jesus Christ is the same as yesterday, today and He will be the same forever, He is and will always be the one to ask the Father for us, just as He asked the Father for the apostles. Our Lord and Savior needs to ask the Father when we make prayer so that the Father will send the Holy Spirit to be with us forever. The Spirit is our comforter, our heavenly guest, and our friend sent by The Father. All the believing Christians must continue praying until the Lord Jesus Christ breathes on us and baptizes us in the Holy Spirit. Because according to John the Baptist, Jesus Christ is the only one who baptizes in the Holy Spirit with power.

Come quickly, Lord Jesus Christ. We are waiting and praying just as the disciples were in the upper room, waiting and praying, and the Holy Spirit descended upon them.

When the day of Pentecost fully arrives, the God

of creation will fulfill His promise, the one He made to Abraham, Isaac, Jacob, the prophets, the disciples, and to us, the people of today.

God, the Father Almighty, never goes back on His word. When He said it, it was done. He said, if heaven and earth are passing away, not one letter, one word, or one jot of his word will pass away without being fulfilled.

The Scripture says: "Do not think that I have come to abolish the Law or the Prophets; I have not come to abolish them but to fulfill them. I tell you the truth until heaven and earth disappear, not the smallest letter, not the least stroke of a pen, will by any means disappear from the Law until everything is accomplished" (Matthew 5:17-18)

Whatever God Almighty planned before the beginning of creation, He will accomplish it by His word and by His power. What God has been saying from the Old Testament through the prophets now comes to reality.

When the day of Pentecost finally arrived, God

poured down his Holy Spirit. The Scripture revealed: "When the day of Pentecost came, they were all together in one place. Suddenly a sound like the blowing of a violent wind came from heaven and filled the whole house where they were sitting. They saw what seemed to be the tongue of fire that separated and came to rest on each of them. All of them were filled with the Holy Spirit and began to speak in other tongues as was divinely ordained before the creation of the universe." (Act 2: 1-4) This is the harvest that the Lord has been talking about from Old Testament to New Testament that will include both Jewish and the Gentiles in the world. It is a worldwide harvest that will include all the inhabitants of the world. It is a day of the beginning of the new heaven and a new earth where God will live among His people. He will be our God, and we will be His people forever and ever.

Our Lord Jesus Christ spent more than three years on earth. During this period, He taught and prepared 12 disciples for the day of Pentecost. It was the beginning of a new era for the universe—a new power rising for prevailing the righteousness of God, a new mission of the completion of the redemptive work of our Lord Jesus Christ, a new way of love and fellowship that flourished God's relationship with our Lord and Savior of all the people on earth. Pentecost was the second great festival of the Jewish year. It was a harvest festival celebrated when the first fruits of the grain were harvested and presented to God. Therefore, Pentecost was a symbol for the church, similar to the body of Christ that marked the beginning of God's harvest of the souls of believing Christians on earth.

There were three observable events on this particular day - the manifestations of the Holy Spirit that descended upon more than one hundred and twenty people, including disciples who were in fulfillment of the promise of the Father, which they had heard from the Son Jesus Christ. (1) An audible manifestation apparent from a violently blowing wind that filled the entire place where the disciples were staying. It was a prophetic sign that showed the Holy Spirit was coming into power. Wind, in particular, is one of the symbols biblically used for the Holy Spirit. This reminded all the believers that the Spirit of God is the active agent for the creation of the earth, and it is active in the act of salvation as well. The Holy Spirit was the gift of God to Jesus Christ, His one and only begotten Son. The Spirit was a gift to the Son, and through Him, it was blessed to the entire universe. The wind, the fire, and the tongues are all manifestations of the Holy Spirit's presence. These are the signs associated with the Holy Spirit and are considered a gift.

(2) There was a visual manifestation of what seemed to be the tongue of fire that rested on each of the disciples as a prophetic symbol. It represented that the Holy Spirit was coming to empower them to be fiery, contagious witnesses for the Lord Jesus Christ. (3) Speech manifestation was prominent as all the followers of Jesus were gathered, including the disciples. They were all filled with the power of the Holy Spirit. They began to speak in other languages as the Spirit enabled them or gave them utterances. They spoke in a variety of native languages, which were understood by the people who had come from

the respective nations.

All the people that had come from different nations understood their language, which the disciples were speaking. They spoke all the foreign languages with a supernatural flow driven by the power of the Holy Spirit. These three-fold manifestations of the Holy Spirit were observable at Pentecost and corresponded exactly to the promise of our risen Lord—the promise He made to His disciples concerning the power to be witnessed by the people all over the earth. The disciples rejoiced that Christ, in His ascended position, as our exalted Lord and Christ, was at the father's right hand of authority. The importance of the Holy Spirit's power marks the beginning of the fulfillment of God's promise in the book of Joel—the promise to pour out His Spirit to all the people in the world.

Everyone was confronted with the decision to repent and believe in Jesus Christ. The disciples were clothed with the power from above, which enabled them to be the witness for Jesus and convey the essence to people through whom the Holy Spirit could bring great conviction to the lost, turning the lost from sin to salvation in Jesus Christ. The people in concern here were the people who were lost in regard to sin, righteousness, and God's judgment.

The Holy Spirit revealed His nature as a Spirit who longs and strives for the salvation of people of all the nations. Those who received the baptism in the Holy Spirit were filled with the Holy Spirit, and they will surely begin longing for the salvation of humanity.

Therefore, Pentecost is the beginning of a world that is concentrated on a mission involving the sinners and the lost. The day of Pentecost brought the people of the world into a new dynamic of light a light that ignites the spark of every human being that comes to the world with the life of righteousness. The Holy Spirit's power brings light into the world of sin and wickedness. It brings light to the world of darkness, ensuring that the darkness cannot overpower it.

On the day of Pentecost, the disciples became the ministers of the Holy Spirit. They preached about Jesus Christ's crucifixion and resurrection. They were leading others to repentance and faith in Christ Jesus. They baptized the sinners and the lost and told them to receive the gift of the Holy Spirit. They encouraged the people to seek the gift that they themselves received at Pentecost. They continued leading others to the baptism of the Holy Spirit. Through the baptism in the Holy Spirit, Christ's followers became the successor to his earthly ministry. They continued to teach, in the power of the Holy Spirit, in continuation with the Lord who started this teaching.

As the manifestation of the Holy Spirit, tongues are the supernatural power of the Holy Spirit. The spirit inspired utterance and enabled the believers to speak in languages that were foreign or unknown. It is one of the gifts of the Holy Spirit to all Christian believers.

On the day of Pentecost, the Lord gave His people His Spirit under the new covenant. On that day, the power to obey the gospel was bestowed upon all the disciples and all those who believe in Jesus Christ by the Holy Spirit. We are no longer under the Law which was written in the stone but in the Spirit. The Spirit writes the precept upon the flesh of our hearts. Jesus Christ ascended into heaven to pour out the power to do the gospel ministry work. The day of Pentecost was the day of the outpouring of the power of the Holy Spirit on those whom the Father chose. From the beginning of creation and before the foundation of the universe, they will all come to Him; no one will be lost.

The Lord will dwell among us to instruct us about all the things that pertain to life. The Lord God will live among His people to a degree higher than ever before; where boundaries were set to keep correct the trembling people. The Lord will dwell in the hearts of His people; He will be present in love and in a good relationship, fellowship, and the indwelling of the power of the Holy Spirit will leads us all to redemption. Pentecost was the day of the inauguration of the gospel of God's dispensation.

On the day of Pentecost, Apostle Peter preached with boldness. He renounced the proclamation of the gospel, spreading the message that Jesus Christ is the coming Messiah. Were being fulfilled in Jesus

Christ on the day of Pentecost, which also marks the beginning of His last days. Jesus is both Lord and Christ, crucified, raised, resurrected, and exalted to the right hand of God. Jesus Christ received the authority to pour out the Holy Spirit to those who believe in Him and gave His life to Him. All the believing Christians must give their lives to Jesus Christ as Lord, repent from their sin, and be baptized in connection with the forgiveness of sins. They should be baptized in the Holy Spirit with faith and repentance. Those who hear in faith must separate themselves from the sinful world and from the corrupt generation.

The Pentecost the pouring of the Holy Spirit upon all the believers is the love of Christ and was a symbol of a new life in Christ. Lord Jesus is our exalted Lord whom King David called "My Lord." He is the one on whom we must call for our salvation. Jesus Christ is the Lord; His name above every name a name that stands for His authority, His holiness, His mercy, His love, and His grace. This name, Jesus Christ, declares the full relation of God to all humanity. Jesus Christ is the name for the Old Testament and Messiah, both of which mean 'Anointed One.'

Pentecost was the evidence on the universe that our Jesus Christ was now exalted as Lord and Christ in heaven and on the earth. The outpouring of the Holy Spirit by Jesus Christ provides that He is indeed the exalted Messiah. He is now sitting at the right hand of God the Father, interceding for all those who belong to Him in the universe. Jesus Christ, now sitting at the right hand of God in the unity of the Holy Spirit lives to continuously pour out the Spirit on all those who believe in Him. While pouring out the Holy Spirit, Christ intends to empower the Christians and motivate them to continue His mission, follow His teachings, and remember whatever he taught them while He was on earth during his earthly ministry.

The Holy Spirit empowered all disciples, so they won many people to Christ. They started the house churches and preached and taught in the Synagogues and Temples. They could do all this because they were energized and empowered by the Holy Spirit on the day of Pentecost. Up till today, without the power of the Holy Spirit in the life of believers, no one can serve the Lord faithfully and sincerely. The outpouring of the Holy Spirit and the accompanying of the supernatural signs cannot be limited to just one day of Pentecost. The power and the blessing of the Holy Spirit are for every believing Christian to have and to experience. It is and will be there throughout the church age and the entire period of time, between Christ's first coming to the world and His second coming.

The day of Pentecost was the day that the Holy Trinity equipped the church with the power of the Holy Spirit so that it would be glorified among the people in all the nations of this world. The words might be filled with the knowledge of the glory of the Lord, but the love of God will surely be manifested in the hearts and minds of the people of this world. People speaking any language or belonging to any nation will bow down before the Savior of all. He is the Lord of all, exalted with prayers, praises, and thankfulness for all that He has done for us and continues to do for us by pouring out His Spirit upon us.

Churches of Jesus Christ will be growing more

and more every day with the outpouring of the Holy Spirit. The repentance and forgiveness will be flowing out of the hearts and minds of the sinners and the lost. All the believing Christians' main purpose and responsibility is to spread the knowledge of the gospel to all the nations, starting from our neighborhood and our community to spreading it to our cities, states, and countries. God's eternal purpose at Pentecost was to equip the saints and the church with the mighty power of the Holy Spirit, indwelling them, so they are able to take the gospel to all the nations. This would bring great glory and honor to His Holy name, resulting in His eternal glory from this earth to heaven.

The Spirit of Jesus Christ that dwells in us will empower us with a strong desire to witness to those who are sinners, the lost, and the perishing and who have never heard about the gospel. The Holy Spirit's power will make us Holy in all the areas of our lives, empowering us in whatever we are doing.

Wherever we go and whatever we say, we will bring glory to God as witnesses to the love of Jesus

Christ to the lost people in this world. The day of Pentecost is one of the significant days in the history of this universe. It is the day that the Spirit of God descended in order to live among His people with power and love, so that the people of the world will be saved from the power of sin and death.

Chapter Sixteen

Jesus Christ's Great Commission Of The Gospel From Disciples To All Christians

The Holy Bible's most important assignment is the great commission. It is the last word of Jesus Christ recorded before his ascension to the Mountain of Olives. The great commission is also a call from Jesus Christ, our Savior, to all who believe in Him. It applies not only to His disciples but also to us, His followers, till the end of time, until He returns to the Earth. The great commission marks the completion of the work of redemption, the ending of the gospel, and the beginning of faith and action. It is an instruction from Jesus Christ to all those who have deep faith in Him and are close to Him. It also applies to all believers who share a close friendship with the Lord. This kind of love spurs because you know they are so good to your heart. Your love makes you want to share the goodness you have received from others. The Bible tells us to "Taste and See How Good Is the Lord."

(Psalm 34:8)

Jesus Christ has given all authority and power to us Christians. He said that He had overcome the world. This is an incredibly powerful and great word from our Lord to His disciples today. It should encourage us to have strong, healthy faith in Him.

The great commission is the commandment of Jesus Christ to His apostles before He went to heaven. He sat at the right hand of God, the Father, and reigned in the unity and power of the Holy Spirit. The great commission is a task. It is an assignment that all Christian believers must fulfill until Christ Jesus, Our Lord returns. Jesus Christ is God, the Son. However, He was also fully human. He fulfilled His ministry on earth with the Holy Spirit. It was through the Holy Spirit that Jesus was anointed as the Son of Man. It was the strength of the Holy Spirit reflected in Jesus Christ so that He was able to live and preach the gospel. All believers in Christ are instructed to follow Jesus Christ's example. Every believer on earth must seek the Spirit Power to live the life Christ desired for His followers. We must adapt the lifestyle that is pleasing in our Lord Jesus' eyes.

The Holy Scripture revealed God's great commandment through Jesus Christ, his Son, and Lord Jesus Christ. He gave us this commandment before his ascension: "Then the 11 disciples went to Galilee to the mountain Jesus had instructed them to. They worshiped him when they saw him; some were skeptical. Jesus appeared to them and stated that He had all authority on earth and heaven. Go therefore and make disciples of all nations. Baptize them in the name and Holy Spirit of the Father, Son, and Holy Spirit. Teach them to follow everything I have commanded them. And I am with your every need, even to the end of the age." (Matthew 28,16-20).

The Lord Jesus Christ spoke to His disciples before His ascension into heaven and offered them a word. That specific speech's objective was to help His followers through His absence it is meant to be a sacred guide before He departed to the other world. He stated that all authority and power on earth and in heaven had been given to Him. God's people have been promised power and authority to spread the gospel around the globe. But first, they must obey Jesus Christ's commandment that they will wait for the promise from the Father, which is the Holy Spirit at Pentecost. We must be given the power to go to all nations. We cannot do this alone.

The Holy Spirit must be present in baptism for all of them. In another Scripture, the Lord stated: "Jesus answered, if anyone loves me, he will follow my teaching. My Father will love him, so we will go to him and make our home together." (John 14: 23).

This means that those who love Jesus Christ and follow His teachings will feel the presence and love of the Father as well as the Son. Through the Holy Spirit, the Father and Son will be revealed to the believers. The Holy Spirit will make Jesus Christ known to faithful Christian believers. He makes it clear that Jesus Christ is present with Him and the one who loves Him. The Holy Spirit will help us to see Jesus in a close proximity and experience His love, blessings, and help. This is the Holy Spirit's first task. We should respond in love to Jesus Christ, worship Him, and give our all to Him because He comes to us through

His Holy Spirit.

The Father's love is associated with our Love for His Son. The attainment of God's love is conditioned upon should be conditioned by our love for Jesus Christ and our loyalty to His Word. We must then be able to recognize that this love is conditional and based on our love and obedience to his Word. Jesus Christ's greatest commission was directed to all of His disciples from every generation. It is a missionary's task to fulfill the goal and the responsibility. It also empowers the objective of commissioning the preaching process of the gospel to churches. The church's mission is to preach the gospel and make sure its message and meaning are delivered to all people, exactly according to the revelation of Jesus Christ. The mission also includes the responsibility to send missionaries to every country. The gospel's message encloses some vital points of our faith and history. Hence it must focus on repentance, the forgiveness of sins, and the promise to receive the Holy Spirit. It also includes the exhortation of Christians to get rid of this corrupt generation while the followers wait for

Christ Jesus, our Lord, from Heaven. The purpose of the gospel is not to convert people but to transform who will follow Christ's instructions into disciples.

It is significant also because this is Christ's only direct directive. Christ's primary intention for evangelism or missionary witness is not to intrude in the decisions regarding conversion. Hence following our Lord's path, we must not focus on expanding congregations or increasing the members of the church, but rather focus on the spiritual evolvement of the people. We must be devoted to spiritual growth and dedicate our energy to disciples who are free from the world and follow Jesus Christ's commands.

Jesus Christ has told all believers to focus on spreading the Word of God. He has taught us to make it our mission to reach sinners and the ungodly men and women of all ages, including children, and show them the light of God. Jesus Christ does not want us to Christianize the world or take over it. Believers must be free from the corrupt world system so that they have the courage to expose all the evil in the world. Those who believe in Jesus Christ are to be baptized with the gospel. They have made a covenant promise to abandon all forms of immorality on the earth. They have sworn to avoid the sinful natures of the world and to fully commit themselves to Jesus Christ, His kingdom's purposes, from this world to heaven.

Jesus Christ will always be present with His faithful, obedient people in the presence of the Holy Spirit. These people are witnesses to all nations only after they have been covered with the power from above. Christ Jesus promised that His authority and presence would always be with those who believe in Him now, and forever, and every day thereafter. Jesus Christ is present with us. He is there in all we do in the name of the gospel to carry forward His Word and the essence of the Holy Spirit. Christ is there for us no matter what the nature of our circumstances. He cares for us in all things, regardless of whether we are weak or strong, rich or poor, sick or healthy, and His grace is more than enough.

His presence will lead us, and he will not leave us. Jesus Christ spoke His truth when He said: "heaven and earth will pass away, but my Words will never pass away " (Matthew 24: 35).

Baptizing in God's name, God the Father, God the Son, God the Holy Spirit, is important because Father, Son, and Holy Spirit are one God. Christian believers should not fear or worry. They must not have doubts when they are in trouble. They must not be discouraged in bleak times. Jesus Christ is always with His people. Christ Jesus, before His crucifixion and resurrection, had authority as the begotten incarnate Son of God. The Father was pleased to grant Jesus Christ all that was in heaven and earth. Christ granted the authority to the disciples and all Christians today to preach the gospel to all people in all nations and under the earth. The great commission does not belong to just the missionary; in fact, it belongs to all the Christians.

All believers must share the gospel with sinners and the unbelievers so that they can become aware of Jesus Christ and that He is their Redeemer King. The Lord Jesus Christ gave believers an assignment, and He gave them power through the Holy Spirit to accomplish the task He had given.

All Christians, followers of Jesus Christ, and believers in Jesus Christ have to follow Christ's commandment to preach, teach, and witness the gospel to all people, especially those from other religions. After the baptism, believers in Jesus Christ are empowered by the Holy Spirit. This gives them the ability to preach, teach and witness the gospel of Jesus Christ. It also strengthens and deepens our relationship with Holy Trinity, Father, Son, and Holy Spirit, for it is through them that we receive the power that fills us with the power to do the work of God. With the enablement of power and spirit through God, we must preach boldly and faithfully. It gives strength to all believers to reach people around the world to be saved and live a holy life as the Lord Jesus demanded from everyone who came to this world. Jesus Christ did not wish anyone to die or to perish. The great commission of His gospel must be fulfilled in every country, mountain, wilderness, and valley, as well as all cities, towns, villages, and caves, before Jesus Christ returns. He wanted them to repent, ask for forgiveness, and come to the knowledge that they are forgiven because of His precious blood on

Calvary.

Christ's power is expressed in the lives and commitments of those who have given their lives to Him. Jesus Christ is the all-powerful, all-knowing, all-compassionate God who reigned in the hearts and minds of all His believers. Jesus Christ's authority in the universe is clear, precise, and perfect. It is here to prevail from beginning to end. All people must hear the good news of Jesus Christ's gospel in every part of the world. Every Christian believer must share the gospel with others in the world. They should start spreading the light of the Lord from their neighborhood and go to the ends of the earth with the same determination and purpose. We should always make it our top priority to spread the gospel and proclaim His honor to all people, no matter where we are, whether we live in another country or move to another state. Christ Jesus spoke his truth, saying: "He will not leave us nor forsake, he's with us always, and forever." (Isaiah 41:10)

We need to remember that Christ is with us everywhere we go and in everything we do for His glory. Millions of people around the globe have heard of Christ's great commission and have welcomed Him into their lives. They have been blessed to experience the trustworthiness in Jesus Christ. The gospel of Jesus Christ is powerful and transforms people from all religions. It helps them worship the true and holy God, the creator and sustainer of the universe. Believers can witness the good news of Jesus Christ's gospel. As believers, we can speak and preach the gospel with peace and power because Christ Jesus has given all power and authority to us. He transferred us the strength in the gospel work. Jesus Christ commands his followers to spread the gospel to all ends of the earth.

This includes baptizing, teaching, and preaching the gospel. All believers must follow the commandment of Jesus Christ and preach, teach, witness, baptize, and call sinners back into Jesus Christ's Holy Hands. Jesus Christ has all power and authority in heaven and earth. He can forgive past and future sins, and He can intercede for the Father on our behalf. He pleads for our case and prays the most powerful prayer we could ever ask. Christ Jesus was granted the authority to send the Holy Ghost to us to help us live for the glory and praise of God the Holy Trinity. Christ Jesus is given the authority to reach heaven and earth, open hearts and minds, move people from darkness to light, make them spiritually awake to worship God in the spirit and truth, and move lost from the dark to the light. Christ can reconcile us with the Father. Jesus Christ has all the authority to grant eternal life to those who have given their lives faithfully and sincerely to Him. Jesus Christ can raise us from the dead and give us the element of immortality that will never let us die.

The most important thing is that Jesus Christ has been given authority in heaven as well as on earth to bring new heaven, new earth a new realm where righteousness dwells. His kingdom will never end, and it will be the ultimate place where God the Holy Trinity one God, will forever live with His people and the world will have no end. Amen!!!

Jesus Christ, the Son of God and the son of Man have been with God from the beginning. He possessed all power and authority. Christ is the mediator between God and man, and all power and authority were given to him through his mediation. Christ was taken to the cross to save us from sin and death. Jesus Christ's bloodshed on the cross has never loose its power to save sinners and the ungodly. It will always pose the power to redeem us from future sins.

For the sake of souls and the salvation of all people on this planet, there is always room at Jesus Christ's feet on the cross until He Himself returns. The ambassadors of Christ are Christian believers; we are His representatives. Jesus Christ, with His authority on earth and heaven, has given us the ministry to reconciliation. We must spread the gospel to all peoples of the planet with the good news about God.

Chapter Seventeen

Christ Ascension Into Heaven In A Bodily Form

The Scriptures revealed that Jesus Christ's ascension to Heaven showed Christ's elevation to God the Father in unity with the Holy Spirit. Our Lord was still alive on earth for 40 days after His resurrection from death. It took place after Easter Sunday. Christ visited His disciples several times during these 40 days following the resurrection to teach and guide them on how to carry on the gospel of God's love. Our Lord ate with them and taught them how to catch fish.

Ascension is the literal word for entering Heaven with a literal body. Even After His suffering, He appeared in front of them and provided them many convincing shreds of evidence that He was still alive. For forty days, he visited the people and spoke of the kingdom of God. While He was having dinner with them, he said to them: "Don't leave Jerusalem but wait for the gift that my Father promised. You have heard me talk about it. John was baptized in water, but within a few days, you will be baptized in the Holy Spirit." (Luke 24:49)

"After He said these words and was immediately taken before their eyes. A cloud covered Him from their view. Everyone stared at the scene as Jesus moved up the sky. As he was moving, they were staring up at the sky when two white men appeared beside them. They asked the men of Galilee why they were standing there looking up at the sky? This same Jesus, who was taken from you into Heaven, will return in the same manner you have seen him go to heaven." (Act 1: 1-5; 9-11).

The Scriptures revealed everything that Jesus Christ did, taught, and preached through the power of God's Holy Spirit. Christ commands His disciples to remain in Jerusalem until they are empowered by the Holy Spirit after our Lord Jesus Christ's resurrection.

"The eleven disciples then went to Galilee to the mountain Jesus told them to. They worshiped him when they saw him, but others doubted. Jesus appeared to them and stated that he had all authority on earth and Heaven. Go, therefore, and make disciples of all nations. Baptize them in the name of the Father, Son, and Holy Spirit. Teach them to follow everything I have taught them. And I assure you, I am with you always, to the end of the age." (Matthew 28: 16-20).

The Lord Jesus, before His ascension into Heaven, told His disciples and followers that all power and authority had been given to Him. All the people of God that exist today or in the past are promised the authority and power to spread the gospel around the globe. They must first obey Christ's instruction to wait for the promise from the Father, which will be revealed through the power and presence of the Holy Spirit at Pentecost. We cannot expect to receive the power that will accompany us in our mission to the nations without following the example of the Holy Spirit's empowerment. All those who have believed in Jesus Christ from generation to generation must abide by His great commissions.

Their goal and responsibility for the commissioning comprise traveling into the world to preach the gospel and teach it to all as per Jesus Christ, our Savior's commandment. This includes the responsibility to send missionaries into every country. Gospel preaching is about repentance, the forgiveness of sins, and the promise to receive the Holy Spirit. It also includes the exhortation not to be corrupt while we wait for Christ's return to earth to establish His kingdom – the kingdom of righteousness and peace. It is not about making converts but rather making disciples who will follow Christ's instructions. This is the sole imperative message in the passage. Jesus did not intend for evangelism or missionary witness to only result in conversion decisions. Spiritual energy should not be used to increase church membership. Instead, it must be used to make, train, and evolve disciples. The element of evangelism must teach the disciples to be free from the world, follow the commands of Jesus Christ, well as following His will with all their heart and mind. Jesus Christ also commanded us to focus on reaching the lost people in the world with pure intention and not prioritized

Christianizing the world or taking control of it.

Believers in Christ must be freed from the evil system of the world and all its immoralities that exist today. The gospel and those who believe in Jesus Christ are to be baptized with waters. Water baptism is their covenant promise to abandon all immoral activities. It includes abandoning the world and sin and fully committing themselves to Christ Jesus and His kingdom's purposes. Jesus Christ will be there with His followers in the power and presence of the Holy Spirit. Only after they have received the power from Heaven will they be allowed to witness to all nations. All who believe in Jesus Christ and follow Him were promised that He would be with them. Jesus Christ promised that His authority and presence would be with all those who traveled into the world to find and train disciples in all nations. Christ is with us through the Holy Spirit and His word. Jesus Christ, regardless of our circumstances, is there to care for us. He watches over us in all our trials, tribulations, and struggles. His presence will bring us home. The great commission is the ultimate responsibility of all

Christians who believe. This is the Christian's solution to all your fears, doubts, problems, heartaches, discouragement, and trouble. Hence, we must be available for Jesus' command before His ascension to Heaven.

Christ's ascension to Heaven was completed, and he is now seated at God the Father Almighty's right hand. Christ's ascension into Heaven in human form signifies the beginning of Jesus Christ's heavenly rule. It also assures us that we will be with Him in His kingdom. Before He was taken from them, Jesus Christ blessed His disciples. God's blessing upon the lives of his people is truly significant for his followers to keep having hope. The blessing of God is a divine gift that will help our work of, ministry work on earth to succeed.

Christ's presence is with us. God gives us strength, power, and all the help we might need to grow. Jesus Christ is always at work in and through us to do good in the world. It is a blessing that God Almighty first did for humanity. God sent Jesus Christ to the world to give us eternal life and the gift to save. We can see the blessings He gave to His children and His followers upon His return from Heaven to earth. The ministry of the apostles is a vital part of the blessing. God's blessings are conditioned in a way that they will be granted if the people choose Him. God's people have to make a decision and decide whether they want to be blessed through obedience or be cursed through disobedience. For His blessings on their ministries, their work, and their families, believers must concentrate on to Jesus Christ. Believers should believe in Jesus Christ, love him, and follow his example.

Everything that could hinder His blessing must be removed from our lives. Christ's ascension communicates Christ's glory. He was returning to His former glory after he won the victory over sins and death. Christ said the following during his priestly prayer: "And now Father, glorify my presence with the glory that I had with you before this world began." (John17.5)

Jesus Christ's prayer of protection, joy, and sanctification for unity is only applicable to specific people; Jesus Christ returns to heaven in Glory and Might. According to the Book of Hebrews, Jesus Christ was made to look like His brothers so that He could be a merciful high priest serving God. (Hebrews 2: 27). Jesus Christ is the mediator and high priest who is merciful and faithful. Jesus is the representative of believers before God, just like the high priest represented Israelites on the Day of Atonement. Jesus Christ's ministry as high priest made atonement for our sins by taking God's wrath off us through His ministry of mediation. We can now call God Abba or Father because we are now able to approach God confidently.

Christ, our high priest, also sympathizes with our temptations and comes to our assistance. He understands our flawed nature. Blessed though is His own sacredness that even though He was a human, He has been through suffering, trials, and temptations; the Christ did not sin. Jesus Christ is our high priest forever. He went to the Holy of Holies once per year to atone for the sins of the Israeli people. Jesus Christ atoned for all people on the planet once. The blood of Jesus Christ saved humanity. The ministry of Jesus Christ as God in Man was ended with His ascension. The church will continue to minister through His words until He returns. The ascension of Jesus Christ sends the Holy Ghost to dwell in all believing Christians. This is the bodily presence of Jesus Christ.

All the apostles and believing Christians around the globe saw the ascension of Christ Jesus as a significant event. It allowed believers to be transformed and advance the gospel through the body of Christ, the church. Ascension marks the end of Jesus Christ's ministry in His bodily form; and brought Him back to the Father's glory from the beginning. It creates a new heaven and earth where righteousness can dwell.

The apostles and all Christian believers have felt profound effects from the ascension of Christ. Jesus Christ was taken to Heaven at the moment when a disciple who didn't believe as Thomas did, but until he saw His hands and feet after, the ascension; he began to worship Him with joy. The ascension and resurrection of Jesus Christ bring joy to all who believe in Him because He sends his Holy Spirit. Jesus Christ ascended and sat at the right side of the Father.

His Father reviewed his achievements of life, death, and resurrection and confirmed that sin's final payment had been made. Christ's ascension opened up the intercessory ministry for all Christians. Christ Jesus is our great Intercessor in Heaven; Christ will always intercede on behalf of His people at God's right hand, forever pleading for our cases and assisting the Father with whatever we need. Jesus' ascension into Heaven made the Holy Spirit enablement possible for all Christians to complete the work Jesus Christ assigned for them to do while waiting for His return back on earth.

Chapter Eighteen

Christ Jesus Is Coming Again To Judge The Dead And The Living

The Scriptures reveal Jesus Christ's second coming: "And if you go and prepare a spot for you, then I will return and take you to be there with me so that you may also be where I am. You know the way to the place where I am going." (Jon 14: 3 - 4)

Jesus Christ will return from heaven. He will return from the Father's presence to take His faithful followers to heaven, which has been prepared specially for them. He will take those who are faithfully following him to heaven to the prepared place. This is the blessed hope for all Christians that has been blessed them with motivation, and it will be the hope for all believers forever. Our Lord's ultimate goal is to bring believers together to see His glory. Christians will be taking out of the world; this means rapture, when all Christians who believe will be gathered in the clouds to meet Him and live forever with Him.

Jesus Christ will be coming for His faithful disciples, which will allow them to escape the trials and tribulations that are ahead. All Jesus' believers; who desire to be with Him forever, and have been waiting for the moment for so long, will find comfort in this glorious and eternal reunion. We must all encourage each other about the return of Christ, for there can be no better news for a believer than the fact that He is coming back.

Christ also said in another scripture: "So you must also be ready, because Christ will come at a time when you don't expect him, and no one knows that hour or day, not the angels in heaven, nor the Son, but the Father. It was the same in Chapter Eighteen Noah's days, and so it will be when the Son of Man comes." (Matthew 24:36-37)

The Son of Man will be as visible from the East as lightning. This is important to understand: If the house owner had known when the thief would arrive, he would have kept an eye on the place and wouldn't have allowed the thieves in. The Son of Man will come in his Father's glory with his angels, and then He'll reward each person according to what he did.

Jesus Christ, our Lord loved us so much that He told us about his second return, which will indeed happen. He is the true Son of Man, the Son of God. He will first pour His Spirit with greater intensity. This Spirit will be accompanied by signs and miracles that will ensure the believers about Christ's exaltation and His kingdom's existence on Earth. Jesus, our Lord, confirmed that only the Father knows when Christ will return; in a greater strength, which will be accompanied by signs and miracles to show Christ's exaltation and his kingdom's existence on earth. Jesus, our Lord, confirmed that only the Father knows when Christ will return. This refers to the time Christ was present on earth.

Christ, Who has returned to heaven in His former glory, knows when He will return. He and the Father are one. Believers in Christ need to be alert because there won't be any warning signs before Christ arrives. They must also be committed to Christ's return at any hour, day, or night. Christ Jesus warned His disciples and us, the people of the present time, to be prepared for His return from heaven. After His return, He would remove His church from the world.

Jesus Christ's unexpected arrival's example can be like the unknown time of the night when the thieves arrive. Therefore, at a time not known is as unpredicted as a thief at the night. Believers must be ready and stay devoted to Him at all times, so they are prepared to receive Him when He returns. We don't know when Jesus Christ will return to His faithful churches. It is unknown and unpredictable.

It is essential to realize that teaching can be understood in two stages. The first is the rapture. In this stage, He will raise His followers from the Earth. The second stage refers to His arrival at the end of this age at an unspecified time to set up His kingdom. This applies to all generations of Christians around the world. "While we wait to the blessed hope, the glorious appearing of God and Savior Jesus Christ." (Titus 2:23)

The verse reflects upon the fullness and blessings of God's gracious favor as well as the joy of living in new bodies that are immortal and will never be subject to decay or corruption.

This blessed hope refers to the glorious appearance of Jesus Christ from heaven, which will occur when He returns to all who belong to Him. The great moment is being waited upon; by believers in faith and purity, with a fervent desire to be faithful and be sincere Christians. So, Christ was crucified once to wipe away the sins and will return a second time. "Not to bear sin but to bring salvation for those who are eagerly waiting for Him." (Hebrew 9: 28)

Jesus Christ will return to this world a second time. It would be just like in the Old Testament when the Israelites waited with great anticipation for their high priest to reappear in the sanctuary so that He could atone for them. Believers, who know that their high priest is in the heavenly sanctuary as their advocate, should wait patiently for his return to complete salvation.

"Look, He's coming with the clouds. Every eye will see him. Even those who pierced his eyes, all peoples on the earth will be saddened by him. It will be so! Amen." (Revelation 1:17)

"Behold! I'm coming soon! My reward is with you, and I'll give each one according to his actions. I am the Alpha, the Omega, the first, the last, the beginning, and the end." (Revelation 22:12-13).

"I am the Alpha, the Omega, says God." (Revelation 1: 8)

Jesus Christ will return. The primary purpose of the revelation is to describe God's triumph; Jesus Christ will establish his kingdom on Earth.

The gospel of Matthew records one of Jesus Christ's longest statements; where Christ gives direct clues and events that will precede His second coming; He also warned the believers that no one can know the precise date and time of His coming back to the world. (Matthew 24: 44, 36, 43; 16:27)

Chapter Nineteen

A New Heaven And A New Earth Where Righteousness Dwell

The Scripture revealed: "Behold, I will create a New Heaven and a New Earth. The former things will not be remembered, nor will they come to mind. But be glad and rejoice forever in what I will create, for I will create Jerusalem to be a delight and its people a joy. I will rejoice over Jerusalem and take delight in my people; the sound of weeping and crying will be heard in it no more. Never again will there be in it an infant who lives but a few days, or an old man who does not live out his years; he who dies at a hundred will be thought a mere youth; he who fails to reach a hundred will be considered accursed."(Isaiah 65:17-20)

The Trinity Father, Son, and Holy Spirit one God forever promised of the New Heaven and a New Earth. This prophecy of the Prophet Isaiah foresees the future of God's kingdom on earth. Prophet Isaiah prophesied the age of eternity where sin and death will precede. Our Lord God Almighty said; there will indeed be a New Heaven and a New Earth.

God Almighty the Holy Trinity one God forever has His plan for this present world as well as for Jerusalem, the City of God. Even though death will still be present in the Messianic kingdom, life expectancy will be much, much longer than it is now. A person who lives for one hundred years will be considered a young adult or youth, and if someone dies at the age of a hundred, they will be considered that something goes wrong in their lives.

In another Scripture it revealed: "As the New Heavens and the New Earth that I make will endure before me, declares the Lord, so will your name and descendants endure. From one New Moon to another and from one Sabbath to another, all mankind will come and bow down before me, says the Lord."(Isaiah 66:22-23)

God, the Holy Trinity, spoke to Prophet Isaiah again,

saying that at the end of the Messianic kingdom, God will create the New Heavens and the New Earth. All those who gave their lives to God will live with Him forever.

In the Book of Revelation, the Scripture revealed: "Then I saw a New Heavens and a New Earth, for the first heaven and the first earth had passed away, and there was no longer any seas. I saw the Holy City, the New Jerusalem, coming down out of heaven from God, prepared as a bride beautifully dressed for her husband. And I heard a loud voice from the throne saying, now the dwelling of God is with men, and he will live with them. They will be his people, and God himself will be with them and be their God. He will wipe every tear from their eyes. There will be no more death or mourning or crying or pain, for the old order of things has passed away. He who was seated on the throne said, I am making everything new! Then he said, write this down, for these words are trustworthy and true." (Revelation 21:1-5)

The final goal of the work of redemption of Jesus Christ for all the redeemed people of this world would be a new transformation for the Earth. It will be what the Trinity wants it to be from the beginning of the creation.

Christ will transform the people of this Earth with the gospel with such intensity that it will bring a time in which Jesus Christ will live with His people, and righteousness will reign in the Holy perfection. In order to erase all the traces of sin, the present Earth will have to witness the destruction. Stars, and galaxies of the stars, the sun, and the seas, and everything inside the seas will be destroyed. Heaven and Earth will be shaken and will vanish like smoke. The stars will be dissolved, and all the elements will be destroyed.

The New Earth will become the dwelling place for both humanity and the Trinity. All those who are redeemed will possess bodies like Jesus' resurrection body. It would be a real, visible, and tangible body, but incorruptible, immortal, and which can never be decay. The New Jerusalem, the City of God, for which Abraham and all the faithful people of God waited, would be built and architected by God. The New

Earth will become God's dwelling place, and He will remain with His people forever. The Holy Trinity will wipe all the tears of the redeemed away from their eyes. The effects of sin and death, such as sorrow, pain, unhappiness, and death, will be gone forever.

All the evil things corrupting the first heaven and earth will completely disappear. Believing Christians, will remember all things worth remembering, they will not remember anything that could cause them sorrow.

God Almighty Himself will declare who will inherit the blessings of the New Heaven and the New Earth. It will be those who faithfully persevered as Jesus Christ's overcomers. Those who did not overcome Satan, sin, and ungodliness will be thrown into the Fiery Lake. There will be no darkness and no night in the New Heaven and the New Earth.

The light of the glory of God will fill the city. It will create a strange state, such that there will be neither night there nor any need for light for the commencement of this new earth. The old earth will pass away.

The blessed presence of God with His people will be proclaimed. It will prove that the presence of God with His people and His church is counted as the glory of the church. The presence of God with His people in heaven will not be interrupted as it gets interrupted on earth, as God will dwell with them forever. In the new blessed Earth, God himself will act as a tender Father. With His kind gentle hand, He shall wipe away tears of His children, whereas, all the causes of future sorrow shall be forever removed. God the Father will fulfill His promise as He said: "He will make all this new."

His honor is a pledge of His full performance. He is the Alpha and Omega, the Beginning and the end. His power and Wills were the first and the end. He will complete what he has designed from the foundation of the earth. His power and His will were the cause of all things; His pleasure and His glory are the last ends. God will prove His greatness and goodness in the life of His people. He will provide and give the water of life freely in the fullness of it. He will be all and all. The believers will enjoy the blessedness; as they are the sons and daughters of God.

As the people of God, they will enjoy communion with the Trinity and will be closer to Him in proximity than they could ever dreamed of, God will be with them in a nearer and dearer relationship; the one and only Who sits on the throne will renew all things.

Make all things new His word is true and faithful, and it will surely come to pass, and be fulfilled. God the Father, Son, and Holy Spirit One God, the Holy Trinity's purpose for this universe on which we live will be brought to completion as He is the creator and decides the object of all creations.

The one who began his work will bring it to completion. He is God eternal, the one who gives the water of life salvation through the gift of grace. He will bless the overcomer with complete inheritance and a new intimacy between Father and the Son.

There will be no sea and the sun in the New Heaven and the New Earth; because the Sea was a raging, threatening, and fearful place that the Lord

Jesus Christ often calmed down when the apostles cried out to him in the boat. Furthermore, the Sea signified chaos, disorder, and evil, for them. It is the home of the dead and is also associated with the place from which the beast comes. Therefore, there will be no sea in the New Heaven and the New Earth because God did not want His children to live in fear, chaos, or death. The Lord God will make everything new.

The New Earth will not be plagued by any power of evil. God's intention and plan from the beginning is to dwell with His people. The New Jerusalem will be the eternal ruling place of Jesus Christ the Holy City that comes down from heaven with God. There, all the people will be Jesus Christ's bride, and they will be redeemed. The dwelling place of God, His Tabernacle, His Temple, and His immediate presence will then be on the New Earth.

The promise that God made to Abraham: "That all nations will be blessed in him will now be fulfilled. It is a provision for every saint, as is their eternal status as God's children. The rightful heirs to all the promises of

God in the Davidic Covenant will have the privileges to rule and have intimacy with Father, Son, and Holy Spirit." Scripture References are:

(Genesis 22:18, and Galatians 3:16)

All believing Christians, the overcomers, who faithfully and sincerely gave their lives to Jesus Christ, the true Son of God, they will by faith and will overcome the world of sin and death as well as their sinful nature by the power of faith.

A New Heaven and a New Earth is a divine vision of judgment and restoration that would serve as the introduction of the New Jerusalem a new creation. It would be the beginning of God's enduring presence with His people.

The people of God must persevere in their faith and stay out of the world of sin and all its sinful nature. A New Heaven and a New Earth is a glorious new creation; as well as the Holy City of Jerusalem and the everlasting heavenly city, which represents God's redeemed people.

God's dwelling place is now among His people. Enduring Fellowship between God and His People would be endured, which was lost in the Garden of Eden. This promise was made possible through Jesus Christ's incarnation. The New Jerusalem will be presented as a glorious Temple City, fulfilling Prophet Isaiah's prophecy and prophet Ezekiel's prophecy as well. God will bring His purpose into completion. He is the author and finisher of our faith. The first three chapters of the Old Testament in the book of Genesis described the creation of the world into the Garden of Eden.

The book of Revelation reveals to us that God is creating a New Earth and a New Heaven. It describes a new creation that excludes all the things that were destroyed in the Garden of Eden. In the New Heaven and the New Earth, there will be no night and no death. Satan will be wiped out to disappear forever; nothing impure will enter the New City. People of God will walk with God again, just as they did in the Garden of Eden before the rebellion of Adam and Eve.

There will be no crying, no pain, no sorrow, and no

death. Once again, human beings will rule over the creations, this time with open access to the tree of life. Everything that was wrong with Adam and Eve's rebellion in the Garden of Eden will be set straight and right in the New Earth. In the Garden of Eden, Adam and Eve were driven out because of disobedience; in the new Heaven and the New Earth, people of God will see God face to face because God will live among them and be their God forever. Amen! Amen! Amen!

Chapter Twenty

Jesus Christ Will Reign Forever And His Kingdom Will Have No End

What we will be doing in heaven? When we get to heaven what shall we be doing? We will be singing songs of praise to the Lord.

According to the Holy Scripture in the book of Revelation: "After this I heard what sounded like the roar of a great multitude in heaven shouting: Hallelujah! Salvation and glory and power belong to our God, for true and just are his judgments. He has condemned the great prostitute who corrupted the earth with her adulteries. He has avenged on her the blood of his servants. And again, they shouted: Hallelujah! The smoke from her goes up forever and ever. The twenty-four elders and the four living creatures fell and worshiped God, who was seated on the throne. And they cried: Amen, Hallelujah! Then a voice came from the throne, saying: Praise our God, all you his servants, you who fear him, both small and great! Then I heard what sounded like a great multitude, like the roar of rushing waters and like loud peals of thunder, shouting: Hallelujah! For our Lord God Almighty reigns! Let us rejoice and be glad and give him glory! For the wedding of the Lamb has come and his bride has made herself ready. Fine linen, bright and clean, was given her to wear. (Fine linen stands for righteous acts of the saints)." (Revelation 19:1-8)

We will shout for joy, sings Hallelujah! Praise, shine, boast of the love of God in our lives, and we will give God the glory for His infinite love for us on this earth.

Hallelujah in the Hebrew language means to praise the Lord. The people of God need to sing praises to his holy name. All the redeemed have been delivered from the power and the penalty of sin and death, but now in heaven through the righteousness and the judgment of God in Christ Jesus; all the believers have been delivered from the very presence of sin and death Hallelujah!

The final and complete shout of songs and praises

will comes from all the redeemed. The Scripture revealed: "Therefore, at the name of Jesus, every knee should bow, in heaven and on earth and under the earth, and every tongue confess that Jesus Christ is the Lord, to the glory of God the Father."(Philippians 2:10-11)

The time for the wedding of the bridegroom has come. The marriage of the Lamb will take place after the judgment seat of Jesus Christ and before his second coming.

All believing Christians and saints on earth must stand before the throne where Christ is seated at the right hand of God. They will stand before Christ with their work, which they did while on earth their righteous work, righteous activities will be tested before they will be ready to be presented to Jesus and his bride. The supper of the Lamb is different from the marriage of the Lamb; this is the second coming of the Lord. The center of attraction will be Jesus Christ, the bridegroom. Christ, who is the Lamb of God; the bride, which is the church; and the people that belongs to the bride and the bridegroom and all those who are invited to the wedding banquet, the last people to be invited, are the people of Israel. The marriage of the Lamb will last for thousand years.

We, the redeemed of the Lord, will serve the Lord in heaven. The Scripture revealed: "No longer will there be any curse. The throne of God and the Lamb will be in the city, and his servants will serve him."(Revelation 22:3)

The new creation of the redeemed will be and stands as a replacement to the Garden of Eden. Yes, paradise will be regained! The original order of God will be restored, with the people who are redeemed, ruling over all the creations with Jesus Christ. The tree of life that was forbidden not to eat from, for Adam and Eve and the river of the water of life that was once guarded by Cherubim with the flaming sword at the garden of Eden, will reappear for the weary pilgrims of the Lord as their future inheritance. All the people of God will have their responsibility before God in heaven, just as He gave us an assignment here on earth, each person will have their ministry work in Heaven as well.

Heaven will be the ultimate experience of fellowship. All the people with Christ Jesus and people that have never met him will be in heaven. All the Christian believers will enjoy an unceasing joy, fellowship, and good relationship with the Father, Son, and the Holy Spirit forever.

They will share the love of God, which dwells in Christ Jesus our Lord. It is the love that reigns with Christ as the King of Kings and the Lord of Lords. Scripture revealed: "And there will be no more night; they need no light of lamp or sun, for the Lord God will be their light, and they will reign forever and ever" (Revelation 22:5) The new creation will return to the Garden of Eden, paradise regained!

The original order will be restored, with the redeemed ruling over all the creation with Jesus Christ. The tree of life and the river of the water of life that was once guarded by the cherubim with the flaming sword at the Garden of Eden will reappear to beckon the weary pilgrims of the Lord to their future inheritance. The Scripture says, in the beginning, "God created", which means He did and He knows exactly why He did.

There is no doubt that He is the only one that can bring a new life out of darkness something out of nothing. The spirit of God is with God from the beginning, hovering over the face of the water.

In the first three days, God works together with His son who is the light of the world. God called Him first and said let there be light, and after that, he called out the water, the sky, and the land into existence by His word. God's plan and His ultimate goal for creation cannot be changed or interrupted. With love, and by the power of His word, the earth was created. All believing Christians must trust in the Trinity activity of love and and its ability.

When we make no sense of our lives, when we turn our lives upside-down, we must trust His divine activity of love. We must keep faith in His blessed power and in the fact that He will make any crooked way straight; because His goodness never fails. God makes something new and remarkable out of nothing by the Word of His mouth. God is always present and always will be. Lets keep calling out the light that signifies the grace of God and His presence in the world that He created.

The Scripture says: "For God, who said, let the light shine out of darkness, made his light shine in our hearts to get us the light of the knowledge of God's glory displayed in the face of Christ." (2nd Corinthians 4:6)

The Scripture teaches us that God does not illuminate people's hearts for the sake of themselves alone. God Almighty the Trinitarian God says that at the beginning of the creation of the universe, He spoke His word, and said let there be light, and let it shine in the darkest world. The same Trinity forever one God shone His light through His knowledge and understanding of the gospel of Jesus Christ, knowledge of repentance and prayer for the forgiveness; which is Christ Jesus our Lord.

The Lord Jesus Christ prevails through those who believe in Christ and gave their lives to Him faithfully and sincerely. Therefore, the work of the trinity, which had started at the beginning of the foundation of the Universe, continues with full effect. The Lord God is the eternal God with his evergreen hands; He will take care of his people. They will live in safety. Their land will yield abundant fruits. The heavens will rain the blessings of the Lord down onto every nations that believes and calls on His holy name continually without ceasing. He will heal their land, and there will be plenty of crops and plenty of food, with clean water to drink for themselves and their animals.

The Word of God is eternal, and it stands forever in heaven. His word is to create a person, a righteous person that will show his goodness and justice in all the nations that do not have the wisdom of God; they will exceed the power of their enemies and false prophets.

All your works are true and righteous; your words give eternal life to all the believers of Christ. Your throne O' Lord was established from creation and will extend to eternity to give eternal life to the people of this world.

The Scripture says: "He has made everything beautiful in its time. He has also set eternity in the heart of men, yet they cannot fathom what God has done from beginning to end."(Ecclesiastes 3:11)

God the Almighty Father has placed an inherent desire for more than just the earthly things, within the human heart. He put eternity in the human's heart from the foundation of the world nobody can understand it completely.

People who are into the world cannot comprehend this phenomenon, but God still bestowed His opportunity upon them in the way that He plans and intends well for the people that belong to Him. The redemptive work of God for His created being is good and he has made everything new in its time, he knows the right time for everything in our lives. All believing Christians must trust in the Lord forever, for the Lord, the Holy Trinity is the eternal rock of our salvation. Our Lord is true and Holy God. He is the living God and our eternal King who created the universe and rules over the earth. One God, forever and ever the people of this earth must worship Him, in true Holiness.

How great you are Lord God Almighty, Father, Son, and Holy Spirit, forever one God. How mighty and powerful are your works everywhere in all the earth. Undoubtedly; your kingdom is eternal, your dominion endures forever, from generation to generation, you are our Lord. Your dominion is an eternal dominion; your kingdom is from generation to generation. Let all the people of this earth adore you and give praise. Let them be thankful to your great holy name from now to eternity. The righteous will inherit eternal life and the evil people will inherit eternal damnation.

Jesus Christ is the eternal word of God. He never has a beginning. Christ is the personal word of God. Christ was and is the Lord Almighty. He is the word of God that became flesh. Just as God the Father spoke and the earth was formed, God spoke and Jesus Christ was formed in the Virgin Mary's womb. Jesus Christ was formed in the Virgin Mary's womb. Jesus Christ enjoys an intimate fellowship with his Father. He always used to go to the mountain to pray to the Lord alone. Jesus Christ is a divine means of spirituality for He is the God in human flesh fully divine yet fully human. The Word was God. He is the creator of the world, Jesus Christ; He is the word of God, and He is the revelation of God.

Jesus Christ is the cause of all creation through Him and for Him, as mentioned in the book of Hebrews. The creative word was only with God; but he was God, the Son of God consubstantial with the Father. The Word was Christ created through the Father, the Word Christ created the world with the Father, the Word Christ created the world with the Father and the Holy Spirit; the world was created through Christ who is Son of God; without Him nothing was created.

Christ was the image of the invisible God. It is the work of the Father through the Son and the Holy Spirit, which manifests the love and the wisdom of God. The creation is the work of the Trinity.

The Holy Spirit is the gift that reflects the Spirit of God to the people of the world to see. The world is created with the infinite love of God the Father, the Son, and the Holy Spirit. God the Father is the first person of the Trinity; Jesus Christ is the second person of the Trinity and is called the Son of God and the Son of Man; and the third person of the Trinity is the Holy Spirit. He is the Lord and the giver of life. According to the scripture, the Spirit of God was moving over the surface of the waters before the earth was created. God the Son, Jesus Christ is the embodiment united in one essence. He is consubstantial, distinct in person with regard to God the Father and God the Holy Spirit, the first and third person of the Trinity.

However, the gift of the Holy Spirit according to the Scripture says: "But the fruit of the Holy Spirit is love, joy, patience, kindness, goodness, faithfulness, gentleness, self-control, perseverance, longsuffering, meekness, humbleness, and obedience. Against such things, there is no law."(Galatians 5:22-23)

The Son of Man was God before the world was made. He is the man in our reality. He is the main Child of God by human instinct; He turned into the Child of Man that He may be brimming with effortlessness, truth, and nobility too.

Trinity Jesus Christ knows how to continue on this Planet. The individuals who trust in Jesus Christ don't just suffer hardships as other individuals of the world do. They win in inconveniences and celebrate because they are in a profound sense past their conditions. They carry on with a sense of euphoria inside, amid the life of hardships, since Jesus Christ is the wellspring of their solidarity. Jesus Christ consistently protects us from the domain of the murkiness of the leaders of this universe, the people of transgression. He shows us the realm of his light and ensures us that no obscurity can overwhelm us. It is because we have been liberated from wrongdoing and passing.

Jesus Christ is the Master of the magnificence of God. He is the one through which all things were made. He is superior. He is the sustainer who holds together the Paradise and the Planet. Jesus Christ is the firstborn and will remain the firstborn ever, over everyone spiritual manifestations. Christ is the one through whom all things have been made. His energy brings things together, and His power supports every cause. He is everything the maker, the sustainer, the top of the congregation, the start, the end, the firstborn. Christ is incomparable. He is larger than life. He is the Ruler and Friend in need of this world, the unparalleled, who is before all things. He is the Master of those who He made. Jesus Christ is the Master and the Guardian angel of all. The sky is the limit for Him in Paradise and on the Planets. He is the Lord, everything being equal, all the public authority and the world governments is on His shoulders.

Chapter Twenty-One

Further Explanation of The Trinity

For those unfamiliar with the concept of the Trinity, the Bible presents three distinct theories on explaining the existence of God. The theories one might consider include Arianism, Pantheism, and the beliefs of the Roman Catholic Church. In addition to these three theories, more definitions can be found in the works of Aquinas, John Chrysostom, Lutherans, and the Evangelical churches. In our discussion, we will focus on the definitions found in the New Testament.

Arianism is the belief that there is no deity independent of God. The worship of nature, animals, and plants is condemned and seen as idolatry. Arianism also says that the Father is God while the Son is the man. This means that the Father has the attributes of God but not the same attributes as the Son has. These ideas; were rejected by the majority of the churches and church councils of the Early Church.

The Arian church was crushed in the first crusade of Henry II, but a revival of this version of the faith occurred when the Netherlands; was absorbed by the Protestant Church. In 1570, the Westminster Assembly softened the teachings of the church and made Arianism allowable as a minority belief in the Christian Church. Though these changes did not completely shake the foundation of the doctrine, they did weaken the authority of Arianism.

Pantheism is the religion of "obeying." This idea is not similar to Arianism. Pantheism teaches that the entire universe and life itself are sacred and do not bear a relationship with any one individual, including God. This is a far-reaching and hardline form of Pantheism that excludes modern-day progressives from the pantheon of gods. Many modern Christians have followed in the footsteps of the early church fathers and have adopted this extreme form of religion.

Theophrastus, the father of the church fathers, said that we are saved not from God but from our sins. He went so far as to say that if God is just, He will spare the upright while he will scorch the unrepentant. He further added that those who are saved are holy, while those who are condemned are accursed. John the Baptist was seen by many as a man of great merit; while Paul, on the other hand, was viewed as a man of no worth. This concept is similar to Arianism, wherein the entire world; are believed to be cursed and only those who are saved from this curse become holy.

Arianism was a minority belief held by a few men of the desert before the movement started among the more elite and educated clergy in the Early Church. Most of the Early Church Fathers rejected the concept of the Trinity, and only the ideas of election and divine omni-benevolence were allowed. However, these ideas have been taken up and given a new life by the ecumenical movements of the Churches. There are many congregations today who are accepting the idea of the Trinity; there is a growing body of Church Fathers who are exegesis and who hold to this view of God's relationship with the Church.

Summary

The universe has its origin the Creator. And the Creator who is the triune God; even though: God the Father planned it, and God the Son carried it out, and God the Holy Spirit empowered it, just as the Spirit of God was hovering over the face of the waters of the earth.

God Almighty Father called the world into existence from nothing. He revealed His omnipotent, omnipresent, and omniscient wisdom and His love in His creation. God called all that He created into existence and maintained their existence; He sustained them with His sustainability power from heaven, from then and to this day. The Holy Trinity, the Lord God, loves every creature He created up to the little Tiny Ant that walks on the ground. If He did not love His creation, He would not have created them. God, the creator of all things, accomplished them according to His will. God created the universe according to His plan for the salvation of the people of the world. The Scripture revealed: "In him, we were also chosen having been predestined according to the plan of him who works out everything in conformity with the purpose of his will, so that we, who were the first to hope in Christ, might be for the praise of his glory."(Ephesians 1:11-12) In another Scripture, we read: "And to make plain to everyone the administration of this mystery, which for ages past was kept hidden in God, who created all things." (Ephesians 3:9)

Furthermore, we read the Nicene Creed in our worship service, which says: "I believe in one God the Father Almighty, maker of heaven and earth and all that is visible and invisible; and in one Lord Jesus Christ, begotten, before all worlds. Begotten, not made, being of one substance with the Father, by whom all things were made; who for us men and our salvation came down from heaven and was incarnate by the Holy Spirit of the Virgin Mary, and was made man and crucified for us under Pontius Pilate. He suffered and was buried; on the third day, he rose again, in accordance to the Scripture, and ascended into heaven, sitting on the right hand of the Father. He shall come again, with glory to judge the dead and the living, whose kingdom shall have no end. And I believe in the Holy Spirit, the Lord, the giver of life, who proceeded from the Father and the Son; who with the Father and the Son together is worshipped and glorified; who spoke through the prophets."

All things were made through Jesus Christ; one Lord Jesus Christ, through whom all the things and through whom all the creatures came into existence. Jesus Christ is the cause of all creation, which became possible through Him and for Him. It is also mentioned in the book of Hebrews that the creative word was only with God, but Jesus is God— the Son of God is consubstantial with the Father. The Word Christ created with the Father; the Word Christ created the world with the Father; the World was created through Him. Christ was the image of the invisible God. It is the work of the Father through the Son and in the Holy Spirit, which manifests the love and the wisdom of God. The creation is the work of the Trinity; the Holy Spirit is the gift of God's Spirit to the people of the world. The world is created with the infinite love of God the Father, the Son, and the Holy Spirit. God the Father is the first person of the Trinity; Jesus Christ is the second person of the Trinity, also called the Son of God and Son of Man; and the third person of the Trinity is the Holy Spirit, the Lord and the Giver of Life.

According to the scripture, the Spirit of God was moving over the earth before it was created. God the Son, Jesus Christ, is the embodiment united in one essence, consubstantial distinct in person to God the Father and God the Holy Spirit, the first and third persons of the Trinity.

The Scripture revealed about the gift of the Holy Spirit: "But the fruit of the Holy Spirit is love, joy, patience, kindness, goodness, faithfulness, gentleness, self-control perseverance, longsuffering, meekness, humbleness, and obedience. Against such things, there is no law." (Galatian 5:22-23)

The Son of Man: He is God before all worlds. He is

the man in our world. He is the only Son of God by human nature. When the Son of God became the Son of Man, He was full of grace, truth, and righteousness as well.

The triune worked at the creation of the world. The Scripture says: "In the beginning, God created the heavens and the earth. The earth was without form and void, and darkness was over the face of the deep. And the Spirit of God was hovering over the face of the waters."(Genesis 1:1-2)

The Biblical understanding of the work of redemption, the heart of which is our Lord and Savior's claim that this life is eternal, is that people must know the only true God and Jesus Christ, whom the triune God sent to teach the meaning of salvation that lies in the Trinity the essential basis for us being redeemed. It is to know the truth that this world was one at the beginning of creation. It was created by a Pearl of infinite wisdom and power, who existed before all things and before all time and before the world. Because of the difference between the Creator and His creation, we realize that God manifests himself to us through His work of redemption. The Holy Spirit moved over the face of the water at the moment of creation, and the Father made all things through the Son. Nothing was created without the knowledge of the Son. The Trinity works together in unity with one purpose and with love. Jesus Christ is one of the Triune God: He has no beginning and no end; Jesus Christ is one with the Father, and He said, "Before Abraham, I Was." Jesus Christ always exists; He existed before all creations of the world. He is in a good relationship with the Father, loving and in obedience with one another. Our Lord said: "My Father works and I work."(John 5:17) We know that the Trinity is always working to make this world a better place to live. And that is why the three of them said, "Let us make man in our own image."(Genesis 1:26) It clearly shows us that the creation is the work of the Father, Son, and the Holy Spirit. None of them has ever worked alone. The only time they were separated was on the cross when the sin of the whole world was placed on Jesus for the work of redemption to be complete.

God the Father so loved the world that He gave His

only begotten Son. According to the Holy Scripture: "For God so loved the world that he gave his one and only Son, that whoever believes in him shall not perish but have eternal life. For God did not send his Son into the world to condemn the world, but to save the world through him. Whoever believes in him is not condemned, but whoever does not believe stands condemned already because he has not believed in the name of God's one and only Son."(John 3:16-18)

The role of the Trinity was specific; each is fully God. The roles within the Trinity are very distinct for each member: God the Father creates, God the Son redeems, and God the Holy Spirit sets apart and empowers. They perform their roles with full cooperation and with unity in each operation; all the three members of the Trinity are always present. God the Father is permanently the Creator, but the Son and the Holy Spirit are also involved. The Scripture says: "For by him all things were created; things in heaven and on earth, visible and invisible, whether thrones or powers or rulers or authorities; all things were created by him and for him. He is before

all things, and in him, all things hold together."
(Colossians 1:16-17) In Jesus Christ all things were
created. He is the firstborn of all creation, which
means that Jesus Christ was a created being. Christ
is the heir and ruler of all creation as the eternal Son.
Apostle Paul made an affirmation of the creative
activities of Jesus Christ. All things, both material and
spiritual, owe their existence to Jesus Christ's work as
the active agent in creation. All things hold together
and are sustained in Christ Jesus.

The Son as the redeemer, God the Father, and the
Holy Spirit sent the Son to redeem the people in the
world. The Holy Spirit is the sanctifier, and the Father
and the Son work together in cooperation. The Son
testifies of the Father, the Father testifies of the Son,
and the Son testifies of the Holy Spirit. A voice from
heaven said, "This is my Son in whom I love; with him,
I am well pleased." (Matthew 3:17) Jesus said: "Jesus
gave them this answer; I tell you the truth, the Son can
do nothing by himself, he can do only what he sees
his Father doing, because whatever the Father does"
the Son also does." (John 5:19) The Son testified of the

Holy Spirit: "But the Counselor, the Holy Spirit, whom the Father will send in my name, will teach you all things and will remind you of everything I have said to you." (John 14:26) The Holy Spirit testified of the Son, as the Scripture reveals: "When the Counselor comes, whom I will send to you from the Father, the Spirit of truth who goes out from the Father, he will testify about me. And you also must testify, for you have been with me from the beginning."(John 15:26-27)

God the Father's plan of redemption began as the Son entered the world in human form. The Scripture revealed: "For God so loved the world that he gave his Son." (John3:16) The Son of God entered the world with the name Jesus; the Holy Spirit entered the world as the Spirit of Jesus Christ—the Spirit of Jesus. Jesus Christ was in His glory in heaven before He came to the world. God the Father spoke Jesus into being in the Virgin Mary's womb; that is why John said: "In the beginning was the Word, and the Word was God. He was with God in the Beginning." (John 1:1-2) The Word of God became flesh and came to dwell among us. All three, the Father, Son, and the Holy Spirit, are one God forever—one in essence. When we read the apostolic creed, we see Father, Son, and the Holy Spirit are always working together in unity of the Holy Spirit. The Trinity is co-equal and co-eternal, even though they have different functions with the Godhead. Each performs their roles with full cooperation, obedience, and love. There is forever one God. When Christ returns and the Father sends him, the Holy Spirit will empower him to set up His kingdom of peace and righteousness on earth.

According to the Old Testament, Jesus Christ worked with the Father and came to earth several times as the Angel of the Lord. The Angel of the Lord was different from the created angels like Angel Gabriel and Angel Michael. The Angel of the Lord always intervened in earthly problems of the people and the people in the Old Testament, such as Hagar and her son Ishmael. He also appeared and spoke to Moses in the Burning Bush; He fed Elijah in the Cave when he ran away from Jezebel; He called Gideon. He always interceded on behalf of the people and rescued them. He called Abraham to use the Ram as a sacrifice instead of Isaac.

The activities of the Angel of the Lord stopped when Christ was born in the manger. After Christ's birth, because He came to the world in human form, He could not be God in human form and the Angel of the Lord at the same time. Throughout His stay as Jesus Christ here on earth, He was the perfect radiation of the Father's glory a complete reflection of the Father. He is never changing; He is unchanging, and He is always the same, full of mercy, love, grace, and truth.

"God the Father Almighty chose us in Christ before the foundation. For He chose us in Him before the creation of the world to be holy and blameless in His sight. In love, he predestined us to be adopted as his sons through Jesus Christ, in accordance with his pleasure and will." (Ephesians 1:4-5) God the Father chose all those who will believe in Christ before the creation of the world. This is the wonderful work of love of God the Father the incomparable and incomprehensible love of God before the foundation of the world. He is the all-knowing, all-powerful, all gracious, merciful, and mighty God the uncontrollable and unchangeable God.

It is essential to our Christian faith that we believe that Jesus Christ was conceived by the power of the Holy Spirit, and Christ was fully divine and fully human. The virgin birth was foretold; in the Old Testament by Prophet Isaiah: "Therefore the Lord himself will give you a sign. The virgin will be with child and will give birth to a son, and will call him Immanuel."(Isaiah 7:14) God breathed on Moses, and He directed Moses to write the book of Genesis, just as the Holy Spirit in the New Testament writes through the Apostles and Christ's followers.

The lives of everyone on this earth have a purpose and a reason, and it is that we are God's workmanship created in His image. We are physically created in the image of God to represent God in this world to be His people. We are also spiritually created in Jesus Christ born of His spirit to live a new life in Christ, lost in His love. God's power and love were revealed from the beginning of the creation, and the plan of His redemptive work was also revealed through Jesus Christ, His incarnate begotten Son.

Till today, we can trust the Trinitarian God's ability to manifest in our lives when we cannot understand what is going on in our lives. We must learn how to trust in His goodness and maintain strong faith in Him. He will turn all our troubles, failures, afflictions, and trials into a greater good and bless us. His purpose will be accomplished in our lives and in the life of those who believe in Him.

All three members of the Trinity were active agents in the creation of the universe. Jesus Christ is also the creator who is always with the Father and who is one with the Father from the foundation of the world. That is why God the Father said: "Let us." It is because the Holy Spirit was also present in the creation; the Spirit was hovering over the face of the earth and waters. God's words were pluralistic from the beginning, which shows that God exists in three different persons. All the Trinitarians work together and glorify one another. Jesus Christ, for example, answers our prayer and brings the glory to the Father because he said: "And I will do whatever you ask in my name, so in order, the Father may be glorified in the Son." (John 14:13) In the same way, Christ prayed during His priestly prayer before His crucifixion: "Father, the time has come. Glorify your Son, that your Son may glorify you." (John 17:1) God Almighty is always being, and he will always be God. He was there before He created the world; He existed before the creation of the world. God said, "Let there be light," telling us of the presence of Jesus Christ, who is the light and life of the world, as the earth was in dense darkness before. God Almighty created what was needed first: the light. Since the earth was full of darkness, God brought light into the darkest world. Jesus Christ is the light of the world. In Jesus Christ, all life dwells. The Father created the water, the sky, the land, the Sun, and the Moon. After that, he saw how beautiful and good His work was. Then, He filled the earth with all the creatures, such as animals, birds, and everything that crawls on the ground; He filled it with moving creatures. He also provided food for those created animals by putting vegetation into place. Therefore, all the creatures have plenty of food to eat.

The Scripture says: "Giving thanks to the Father, who has qualified you to share in the inheritance of the saints in the kingdom of light. For he has rescued us from the dominion of darkness and brought us into the kingdom of the Son he loves, in whom we have redemption, the forgiveness of sins. He is the image of the invisible God, the firstborn of all creations. For by him all things were created; this in heaven and on earth, visible and invisible, whether thrones or powers or rulers or authorities; all things were created by him and for him. He is before all things, and in him, all things hold together." (Colossians 1:12-17)

All Christian believers who faithfully and sincerely put themselves in the wisdom of the Trinity know how to persevere on this Earth. Those who believe in Jesus Christ do not only endure trials and tribulations as the people of the world do, but they also triumph in troubles and rejoice because they are spiritually strong beyond their circumstances. They live a joyful life amid difficulties because Jesus Christ is the only source of their strength. Jesus Christ always rescues us from the dark dominion of the rulers of this world of sin and places us in the kingdom of His light that no darkness can overpower. In this kingdom, the believers are free from sin and death.

Jesus Christ is the Lord, the glory of God; He is the one that all things were created for, and He is the sustainer in whom all this holds together in heaven and on earth. Jesus Christ is the firstborn of all creations. Christ is the one in whom all things have been created; Christ is the one in whom all things have been sustained a unifying factor. He is everything the creator, the sustainer, the head of the church, the beginning, the end, and the firstborn. Christ has supremacy over all life; He is the Lord and Savior of this world, the one and only one before all things. He is the Lord of those He created; Jesus Christ is the Lord of all and the Savior of all. Nothing is impossible for Him in heaven and on earth. He is the King of all nations, whose all the government is upon his shoulders.

The Holy Spirit was first mentioned as part of the Trinity when the scripture said, "The Spirit of God was hovering over the Waters." (Genesis 1:2b) He existed from eternity past. People believe that Jesus Christ is the Angel of the Lord before he came down from heaven as a baby in the Manger. The Scripture Revealed: "Oh, the depth of the riches of the wisdom and knowledge of God! How unsearchable his judgments and his paths beyond tracing out! Who has known the mind of the Lord? Or who has been his counselor? Who has ever given to God, that God should repay them? For from him and through him and for him are all things. To him be the glory forever! Amen." (Romans 11: 33-36)

God brings light into the darkest world; Jesus Christ is the light of the world; in Christ, all life dwells.

All Denominational Apostolic Creed/ Nicene For All People

"I believe in God the Father the Almighty, the Maker of Heaven and the Earth, and of all that is seen and unseen. I believe in Our Lord Jesus Christ, the true Son of God, the only eternally begotten not created of the Father, the God from God, the light from light, the true light that shines forever, and no darkness can comprehend it. He is the true God, the very God, one with the Father. Through the Son, all things were created—things in Heaven and things on Earth. He came down from Heaven for our salvation by the power of the Holy Spirit. He became incarnate from the Virgin Mary and was conceived by the Holy Spirit, born of Virgin Mary, and was made man. He suffered at the hands of Pontius Pilate; He was crucified; He suffered death and was buried. On the third day, He was raised from the dead according to the power of God the Father, who called Him out of the grave. He ascended into

Heaven and was seated at the right hand of God the Father. He is coming back in glory to judge the dead and the living, and all the eyes shall see Him; His kingdom on Earth will have no end. I believe in the Holy Spirit, the giver of life who proceeds from the Father and the Son the Holy Trinity with the Father and the Son. He is worshiped and glorified. The Holy Spirit has spoken from the beginning of creation through the prophets and Moses. I believe in the communion of Saints. I acknowledge one baptism for the remission of sins, the resurrection of the body, and life everlasting. Amen, Amen, Amen.

History of Apostolic Creed

The Apostolic Creed is used as an integral form of worship in many universal churches. The Apostolic Creed is recited weekly in thousands of churches all over the world. It was started especially by the Roman Catholic, Protestant, Presbyterian, and all other churches. It created and brought unity to the early churches. The Nicene and Apostles' Creeds are recited weekly in churches all over the world.

When Constantine was in control of the Roman Empire during 312 A.D., he elevated Christianity and brought unity. He held a convention in the year 325 AD in the City of Nicaea. Out of the convention came the Nicene Creed, which is still a standard belief in many churches today. All the Universal denominational churches have a different version of the Apostles' Creed, which was started in a letter by the council of Milan in 390 A.D. Both the Nicene and Apostles' Creed are slightly different, but they affirmed the same Word of God and beliefs. They refer to the

Universal Church as all the body of Jesus Christ on Earth, not the denomination. It is an early word of all the believing Christians and in all denominations based on Christian theological understanding of the Gospel from the Old Testament to the New Testament. It is a belief that was worldwide in the 4th Century under the inspiration of the Holy Spirit.

The Apostolic Creed is very essential for the worship of Saints of the Lord and to read every week, especially during the Sunday worship, as well as every time that the mind suffers in sadness, sorrow, affliction, rejection, and oppression, and all the earthly troubles. It is a great source of strength or source of reflection that will help Christians to be able to stand firmly on the Rock of Jesus Christ our Savior. It has been handed down from the early Christians, but many churches think that it is no longer necessary to read it anymore. It is an affirmation of every believer's faith in Jesus Christ. While reading, some people may decide to use "I" Instead of using "We;" they can do so for more strengthening or to focus their heart and mind on

God by faith.

The Lord's Prayer

The Scripture revealed when the Apostle asked the Lord to teach them how to pray, the Lord Jesus Christ answered:

"This, then, is how you should pray:

"Our Father which art n heaven, Hallowed be your name,

your kingdom come, you will be done

on earth as it is heaven. Give us today our daily bread.

Forgive us our debts, as we also have forgiven our Debtors.

And lead us not into temptation,

But deliver us from the evil." For thine is the kingdom, and the power, and the glory,

Forever and ever. Amen (Matthew 6: 9-13)

Prayer

In the book of Psalms, the psalmists pray this powerful prayer in Psalm 111, which says: "Praise the Lord. I will extol the Lord with all my heart in the council of the upright and in the assembly. Great are the works of the Lord; they are pondered by all who delight in them. Glorious and majestic are his deeds, and the righteousness endures forever. He provides food for those who fear him; he remembers his covenant forever. He has shown his people the power of his works, giving them the lands of other nations. The works of his hands are faithful and just; all his precepts are trustworthy. They are steadfast forever and ever, done in faithfulness and uprightness. He provided redemption for his people; he ordained his covenant forever holy and awesome is his name. The fear of the Lord is the beginning of wisdom; all who follow his precepts have a good understanding. To him belongs eternal praise." (Psalm 111:1-10)

This prayer of the Psalmist emphasizes God's work in creation, His providence, and His grace. I pray that people of this world will seek the knowledge of God's love, wisdom, and understanding of the triune God; from the beginning of the creation of the world. Those who do not know God are foolish in heart and ignorant of their existence. The fiery evil in the world can be removed or reduced by the work of God in creation as well as in sustaining the universe. The Psalmist wants the people to praise the Lord with their whole hearts and flame their hearts with praises and thankfulness. King David praised God with his heart and soul in all that he did throughout his life; we must do the same. We must engage our spirit, soul, body, heart, and mind with praises for what God the Holy Trinity has done, is doing, and what he will do in the years to come in this world. Nothing should be more fitting and more valuable than callings on the Lord's name with praises for joy every day of our lives in everything we are doing.

We thank you, Father, that you are always there for us, in persecution, trials, afflictions, tribulations troubles, and especially when we don't know what to do or where to turn. You always show us the way because you are the way, the truth, and the life. Help us to continue to follow you and abide in your Word. Strengthen us in all the areas of our lives; you are the source of our strength, our stronghold, and our fortress. Thank you for your full presence in our lives; thank you for being the way, the truth, and the life. Let the generation of the righteous of the world be blessed. We praise you with our whole heart Lord God Almighty. We lift our hearts to you; we sing and shout Hallelujah. We give you great thanks for the work of redemption of the people of this world. Help us proclaim your mighty work to the people of this earth who do not know you, our Lord. All glory, honor, and majesty belong to you, our one and only compassionate, gracious, loving God. Answer our prayers when we call on your holy name; help us knock on the door, and open a great door of the gospel ministry in so many ways for us in all the nations of the world. Help us to seek you and find you, let all those who believe in you rejoice in you, let our Soul magnify you, and let our spirit rejoice in God our

Savior. You have done a great thing in our lives; holy is your name forever. You heal the sick, feed the poor, shelter the homeless, and comfort those who are living in fear, in sorrow, and in grief. Bless them with the peace that surpasses all understanding. You have redeemed the people of this world through your Son Jesus Christ, our Lord and Savior and our Redeemer King. You sent your Spirit and touched our hearts with the Holy Spirit's power so that we can approach the throne of grace with confidence for what we need and with whatever we may be going through in our lives. Your Holy Spirit helps us understand and see the world you created, continuously feeling us with your great compassion because you are a compassionate God full of truth and righteousness, abounding in love and forgiveness; we praise you our Lord. Help us always to praise you in the corner of our room and whenever the need is, and to praise you in the congregation of assemblies, in family gatherings with our children praises and adoration whenever time requires and permits us to do so. Help us feel your presence in our lives and say, "Come Lord Jesus, our blessed hope of glory."

This is a good Psalm with an appealing testimony and thanksgiving to the God Almighty Father, Son, and the Holy Spirit. The psalm encourages all the people of God to offer thanksgiving, glory, and majesty to God for all His works and for all that He has done, from our daily bread to His redeeming love for humanity and all His created beings. We must love God more and more as well as live in His knowledge and wisdom to do the work that He has assigned for us to do for Him. It is one of the psalms that says Hallelujah, which means to praise the Lord. All other psalms play an important role by starting with praises to the Lord. By saying praise, the Lord gives us the sense of fellowship and heartfelt religious happiness in the assembling of the righteous. The main focus of thanksgiving is based on what God has done in the past, is doing in the present, and what he will continue to perform in the future. We pray for the Spirit of obedience and praise with thankfulness in our life as we live on this earth for His glory. We pray that the people will come to the knowledge and understanding of the Scripture and give their hearts to you in repentance of their sins and pray for the forgiveness of sins and the resurrection of the body which is only in you. Pray for us, the prayer that you know we need, which will help us to live our life for you faithfully and sincerely. We give you praises and thankfulness for everything that you consistently and faithfully do in our lives so that we may live according to your commandment and according to your Word, without going back to the world of sin and death. Help us to continue applying these psalms to our daily life. In Jesus Christ Holy Name I pray, A Name above all Names in heaven and on earth. Amen! Amen! Amen!

Song Of Praise

The great creator of the worlds, the sovereign God of heaven, His Holy and immortal truth to all on earth hath given.

He sent no angel of his host to bear this mighty word, but him through whom the worlds were made, the everlasting Lord...

He sent him not in wrath and power, but grace and peace to bring; in kindness, as a king might send his son, himself a king.

He sent him down as sending God; in flesh, to us, he came; as one with us, he dwelt with us, and bore a human name.

He came as Savior to his own, the way of love he trod; he came to win us by goodwill, for force is not of God.

Not to oppress, but to summon all their truest life to find, in love God sent his Son to save, not to condemn mankind. Amen!

Words Of The Song By: F. Bland Tucker 1895-1084
Music: Tallis Ordinal, Thomas Tallis 1505-1585

Holy Bible Scripture References:

New International Vision

Bible Concordance

Biblical Index

Genesis 1:1-3; 1:27-31; 1:3-4; 1:2; 1:26; 1:1-2; 2:2-3; 3:8-14; 10:30-32; 11:1-9; 3:22-24; 18:1-15; 21:1-7; 14:17-24; 32:22-32; 3:24; 1:1-2

Psalm 19:1-4; 8:1-6; 33:6; 104:30; 33:6; 110:4; 111:1-10

Revelation 21:1-3; 1:7,2:12-13; 21:1-5

John 1:1-5; 17:5; 14:13; 14:15; 5:17; 3:16-17; 15:17-21; 1:1-5;14:25-27; 1:3; 17:24;1:1-5; 3:16-19;3:1-8;4:7-14;9:1-7;14:25;17:5;14:16-18,26;20:21-23;16:13-15;16:7-11;14:3-4;5:17;3:16-18;5:19;14:26;15:26-27;1:1-2;14:13;17:1

Colossians 1:15-17; 1:15-17; 1:15-17; 1:16-17; 1:12-17

Job 33:4

Ezekiel 37:1-10

Luke 1:26-35; 1:26-37; 2:4,26, 20; 2:21-29,33-39;2:41-52;3:21-23;4:1-15;4:16-19;4:20-21;4:43-44;11:1-2a,3-4,14,21-27,33-36;11:38-44;23:50-54;24:1-10;24:49

Matthew 28:18-20; 2:1-5,9-12; 9:18-25;8:16-17;17:1-8;24:35; 28:16-20; 5:15;5:17-28;24:44,36, 43, 16:27;3:17

Mark 1:3; 10:46-52

Hebrews 1:3; 1:1-3; 6:19-20; 7:1-7; 1:1-3; 1:1-3; 2:17; 9:28

Daniel 3:1-3; 3:7-30

Zechariah 4:6;

Isaiah 7:14; 53:10-12; 32:15; 65:17-20; 66:22-23; 7:14;

1st Corinthians 14:24-26;

2nd Peter 2:17

Romans 4:25; 8:11; 10:9-10

Acts 1:1-5, 9-11;1:14;

Joel 2:28-29

Titus 2:13;

Philippians 2:10-11

Ecclesiastes 3:11

Ephesians 1:11-12; 3:9; 1:4-5

Bibliography

The Student Bible New Revised Standard Version by Philip Yancey and Tim Stafford Zondervan Corporation 1994, 1996 Grand Rapids, Michigan 49530 USA.

Evangelical Dictionary of Biblical Theology Walter A. Elwell Published by Baker Books a Division of Baker Book House Company Grand Rapids, Michigan 49516-6287.

Matthew Henry's Commentary in One Volume Zondervan Publishing House A Division of Harper Collins Publishers Rev. Leslie F. Church, Ph.D. Hist.S. Marshall, Morgan, and Scott Ltd 1960 Grand Rapids, Michigan 49530.

Holman Bible Dictionary. Holman Bible Publishers, 1991.

Horsley, Richard. Bandits, Prophets, and Messiahs.

Harrisburg: Trinity Press International, 1999.

The Message and the Kingdom. Minneapolis: Fortress Press, 2002.

Maier, Paul. Josephus The Essential Works. Grand Rapids: Kregel Publications, 1988.

Martin, Ernest. The Temples that Jerusalem Forgot.

Portland: ASK Publications.

Stegemann, Ekkehard, and Wolfgang Stegemann. The Jesus Movement. Minneapolis: Fortress Press, 1999.

The Archaeological Study Bible. Grand Rapids: Zondervan, 2005.

The Christians Their First Two Thousand Years, Vol. 1.

Canada: Christian Millennial History Project, Inc., 2002.

Wright, N.T. Jesus and the Victory of God. Minneapolis: Fortress Press, 1996.

The New Testament and   the People of God.

Minneapolis: Fortress Press, 1992.

Believer's Bible Commentary a Complete Bible Commentary in One Volume William MacDonald, Art Farstad, 1979, Thomas Nelson Publishers Nashville Tennessee.

Systematic Theology Volume Four Church Last Things Dr. Norman Geisler, 2005 Bethany House Minneapolis, Minnesota.

The Christians Their First Two Thousand Years, Vol. 1.

Canada: Christian Millennial History Project, Inc., 2002.

Wright, N.T. Jesus and the Victory of God. Minneapolis: Fortress Press, 1996.

The New Testament and the People of God. Minneapolis: Fortress Press, 1992.

Believer's Bible Commentary a Complete Bible Commentary in One Volume William MacDonald, Art Farstad 1979 Thomas Nelson Publishers Nashville Tennessee

Systematic Theology Volume Four Church Last Things Dr. Norman Geisler, 2005 Bethany House Minneapolis, Minnesota.

Prophetic Words

"For this reason, ever since I heard about your faith in the Lord Jesus and your love for all the saints, I have not stopped giving thanks for you, remembering you in my prayers. I keep asking that the God of Our Lord Jesus Christ, the glorious Father, may give you the Spirit of wisdom and revelation. So that you may know Him better. I also pray that the eyes of your heart may be enlightened so that you may know the hope to which He has called you, the riches of His glorious inheritance in the saints, and His incomparably great power for us who believe. That power is like the working of His mighty strength." (Ephesians1:15-19)

Lord Jesus Christ, do not let the spreading of the Gospel rest or cease throughout the world. Let your truth continue to be proclaimed until all the people of this world eat the bread of the Gospel, so and they are blessed. They will see the light, know the truth, and set free from sin and death; each soul will see and taste your salvation and receive eternal life, which is only in You.

All believing Christians must learn how to pray for each other. We must be able to ask for God's highest desires for all the believers in Jesus Christ, and especially pray for the empowerment, endowment, and the manifestation of the Holy Spirit from Heaven.

Books Published By Grace Religious Books

Publishing & Distributors, Inc. NY:

- Christ The Consummation of Peace Forever
- Jesus Christ, The Joy of Christmas
- Christ's Life In The Life of Christians
- Christian Cell Phone Godly Wisdom
- The Cross And The Crucifixion
- Be Holy For I Am Holy
- Me I and My Father are ONE
- He Who Believes In Me Shall Never Die
- Jesus Christ, The Only Way to Heaven
- Jesus Christ, The Only Truth
- Jesus Christ, The Only Life
- Light From Heaven Daily Devotional & Songs Of Praises
- Light From Heaven Daily Devotional Study Guide etc.

Read : Gracereligiousbookspublishers.com

Books From the Author World Wide Sellers

Grace Religious Books Publishing & Distributor Inc.

 New York Online Stores

Amazon Books Online Store

Create Space Website Online Store

Barns & Noble

Smash Words.Com eBooks

World Wide Books Stores

Ingram/Spark world Wide Books Distributors

NOTES

NOTES

NOTES

304

NOTES

305

NOTES

www.ingramcontent.com/pod-product-compliance
Lightning Source LLC
Chambersburg PA
CBHW071132180726

48291CB00007B/2150